BEL THE LAST DRAGON
JUNGLES of HABBIEL

JOHN BALTISBERGER

A Splatterpulp Book
From Kaiju Poet Publications

This edition was written and self published by John Baltisberger.

Copyright © 2022 John Baltisberger

Cover Art by Kim Diaz Holm
Edited by Lisa Tone

First Edition
www.kaijupoet.com

Dedicated to my brother Lucas, who is more of a badass than I'll ever be.

The City-East-of-Nod

I

The world was a riot of light and sound. Fireworks rained multicolored flames down, briefly illuminating and reflecting light off the ceiling of stones and stalactites that made up the sky of the City East-of-Nod. The cavernous depths were alive with color and life, the sounds of celebration echoing from one end of the subterranean kingdom to the next. The man stood on an outcropping of buildings carved into the stone, dark orange eyes scanning the jubilant celebration going on throughout the City. Banners of shimmering prismatic colors draped across homes and stalls down in the chaos, and everywhere he looked, there seemed to be some new form of chaotic joy.

By contrast, the man was a study in stoic blandness. He wore an old uniform of blue wool so stained with dirt, dust, and blood as to look more like the gray of the enemy's of his last combat. Dried black blood cracked when he blinked; his face was caked with the stuff, making it look as though he were trying to hide his identity behind a mask of black. He had woken to the cacophony in a city he knew but did not recognize, his last memories of a battle on another continent, of struggling to breathe even as his foe's thumbs dug into his eye sockets … The man reached up, his hands coated in dirt and dried blood, and touched his eye lids, as though to confirm that his eyes were in his skull. He looked away from the City and at his fingers. The dirt under his nails bothered him—more than the blood and more than the stale stench of sweat and ages that wafted from the clothes he wore. He was reborn. That he lived again was not entirely surprising, though not entirely expected either. The man had gambled with his life and lost. To be once again walking was nothing short of miraculous, even for a being with whom mortality had such little meaning. He pulled an Arkansas toothpick from a sheath on his belt and began digging the dirt from under his nails.

He was stalling. Even without the benefit of direct knowledge, he could feel the weight of the years that had passed since he'd walked in the world of the living. At the very least, decades had passed, though more likely, centuries had come and gone. Centuries absent during a war. Who knew who still lived; who knew how the powers of the City East-of-Nod had shifted and what politics were at play now? The man's orange eyes lifted from his fingernails and touched on the palace located at the center of the City. Did the prince of the Sheydim still live? Was the pandemonium of the plethora of demons and spirits below a sign that no hand guided the City? It would not be the first time he was away from what passed for his own kind for so long, but it was the first time that the separation was not by choice. He supposed he had procrastinated enough; he needed answers that would not be discovered under his fingernails.

He replaced the knife at his belt and stepped from the ledge, plummeting the ten stories down to the ground below. The wind tore at him as if eager to rip the costume of humanity away. He hugged himself tight, keeping his blue coat close to his skin as he plunged down to the stalagmites. He landed, his legs bending to take the weight of his speed. Even still, the sounds of his feet hitting the ground after reaching near terminal velocity was deafening. Nearby, a couple of younger beings jumped at the noise.

"Yo, man!" complained a male. His skin was greenish, and the mangle of teeth jutting from his mouth made him look more like a boar that anything that should be bipedal.

A young woman with fire for hair and fine porcelain features had been on her knees before the boy, and she stood, wiping her mouth. She didn't seem self-conscious, just startled. "You okay, man?" she asked.

The man regarded the two younger Sheydim for a moment.

"Fine, just turned around. There is a celebration …"

"Yeah" the boy said as the kids looked at one another, trying to figure out who this strange man was, where he had come from, and how he didn't know what was going on. The male tucked himself back into his pants before stepping forward and smiling at his partner. "Yeah, there is. Things are going …" He paused "Well, we killed another one."

The man stared at him, the intensity in his orange eyes causing the younger Sheyd pause. He stepped in front of his partner, feeling like he should protect her, though he didn't know what from.

"We killed another one, another what?" The man asked. "I have been gone for a very long time. Who did … *we* … kill?" He could tell the kids were afraid of him. This at least, he was used to, the fear, even from his own kind. These were not his peers;

so few of the Sheydim could count themselves his equal. He lifted his eyes towards the palace as he waited for an answer.

"One of them." The girl's voice was not panicked; she sounded proud, as though she were proud to be a Sheyd alive at this time. That was new. There was a deep shame for most of the half-born, baked into their very nature. This pride in a people was almost refreshing. She thrust her bare chest out, heedless of the cool subterranean air. "One of the Watchers."

The man didn't respond. That couldn't be true, it couldn't possibly be true. The Watchers were immortal in a way that even the Sheydim and all the demons of the City East-of-Nod couldn't claim.

"What is your name?" he finally asked the young woman.

"Shaiv."

"Bel," he responded in kind.

"Oh, were you named after the hero from that statue?"

For some reason, Bel found this particularly funny. For the first time since he had woken up, he smiled. He smiled and then laughed hard at the question, hard enough that he had to steady himself on a nearby wall.

"No, I was not named after the statue," he finally managed to respond. "Wait, you said another ...

how many? How many of the Grigori have we sent back to Sheol?"

The woman answered him; her man was still scared of Bel's intensity—maybe he even began to understand who he was talking to. "Three, I think. Wait, no, four, four have been killed." She kept using that word, but Bel was sure she meant captured, sent back to the prison which Enoch had strapped them to so close to the beginning of time as to be meaningless to any creature younger.

Bel nodded his thanks and began walking away from the couple.

"Have a good night, Bel!" the woman called after him.

"Enjoy yourselves" he called back, suddenly feeling in better spirits than he had felt since … well, since before Queen Lillith had begun the war in earnest. There was so much to catch up on, to discover, to enjoy. But first, he would visit the palace and find out for himself exactly what had happened since he was murdered.

Bel strode with purpose. The City was filled with life and unlife, as it had always been. All around him, Sheydim sung and laughed in great revelry. It made sense now; the war that had killed him was still going on, not that he had expected it to ever end. The enemy were as invincible as they were insidious. But the fact that certain members of the order of Grigori had been sent back to their prison was absolutely a sweet nectar that Bel felt he would be able to sup on for years to come.

Everywhere he turned his dark orange eyes, he saw the strange variety of life that were the Sheydim. Given only half form by the Creator, the Sheydim by and large chose their day-to-day appearance, haphazard flittering opinions and whims twisting the appearance of the younger entities, with only habit bearing any true weight and permanence to the creatures. Bel, for his part, had chosen a human appearance back in Macedonia. At the time, it had been novel—most of his peers had taken a look from the cradle of life, looking to mimic their prince and queen. It had been his little defiance against the order of things, a statement of independence. Even back then, he was fighting the war, though in a time when his prince was slumbering and Lillith commanded the hordes of Sheydim into action.

He had taken spear and shield to lead three hundred of his brethren against conquering forces of Amaros that swept out of Persia, seeking to conquer the world once again for their despicable empire of sensation. It had been bloody. Even back in those early days, he had been one of the last of his kind, the rest torn apart in earlier conflicts and killed by human heroes, the very humanity he had been fighting for, for eons. Bel's face was a pale cracked thing beneath the crust of grime and dried blood. A mask of bone behind an impressive black beard. He wore the skin just as he wore the clothes, a disguise for infiltrating humanity on their behalf. His eyes burned in the darkness of the alleyways, ever fixed on his destination.

Several Sheydim stopped in their revelry to gaze at the haggard looking Bel. Everything about him was dull and subdued compared to his surroundings, but still he radiated an undeniable power. Here and there, he saw the shadows of Dybbukim—human ghosts who had nowhere else to haunt and so were drawn to this place to stay hidden from the wheel of life and death until a time they came to accept it. The most raucous of celebrants where neither Sheydim or Dybbukim but the demons—Malikim and Lillikim. Those twisted beings born of unnatural unions. These were the leftover progeny of beings that should never procreate together, Lillith's nonhuman descendants and things created outside of the Creator but using its power.

There had once been a war, even older than the War of Dictates, when the demons had attempted to wrest power away from Prince Ashmandai. It had failed. It was odd to see such strange creatures as these free in the City, given apparently equal status to the Sheydim citizens. For creatures as long lived as the immortal denizens of the City, grudges were usually not so easily forgotten, though that particular war had ended hundreds of years ago at this point. Still, race relations between the three groups had not smoothed over when he had last walked these streets. Perhaps it had been the decades of war against an even greater foe that had driven them together.

Bel watched a traipsing succubus giggle as she plopped down on a window sill and retold some story to a group of friends in front of a stall selling food.

The City East-of-Nod tended to keep up with the times. Humans thought of demons and supernatural creatures as being trapped in the medieval centuries, but the Sheydim did all they could to keep abreast humans. Despite access to magic and powers beyond humanity's comprehension, the Sheydim were still jealous younger siblings desperate to be equals.

Bel's stomach lurched. He had not eaten in centuries, though how long he had been asleep with a corporeal form, he didn't know, not yet. Hopefully, someone in the palace would be able to answer that. He approached the stand the demons were gathered around, the smell of cooking meat and fresh bread drawing him over, waylaying his sense of urgency for the moment.

He ignored the group as his eyes moved over the menu above the stall. He didn't recognize a single item, the ingredients all made sense but not the actual dishes. He realized he had been standing in silence for some time when the voice broke through his concentration.

"You aight, old man?"

"Jojo! That's disrespectful! He's obviously been through some shit."

"Besides, he's probably not even that old, probably just likes the way old dudes look."

Bel turned his eyes towards the three demons. They wore bright clothes with no buttons but metal teeth that kept what little they wore on. Strappy things with studs and leather. It reminded him of a mix of the berserker barbarians and Persian harems all at once. The one identified as JoJo was a squat satyr, his goatee braided with bits of gold and emerald. His goat eyes examined Bel curiously.

"Okay, fine, he does look like shit, Dara," he retorted. "I mean, what's up with those clothes? Boring as fuck."

Dara, the succubus with hair that could only be described as electric blue, rolled her eyes. "Sorry about JoJo, mister; he's mad because his mom forgot to teach him manners."

Bel grunted, meeting the satyr's eyes. Bel had known the horrid little creatures in olden times, when they had served first the sexual whims of the Grigori and then went on to serve other powerful beings as harbingers of lust. This JoJo was probably in a foul mood because here in the City East-of-Nod, he would be unable to satiate his desire for human flesh.

The third speaker, a one-eyed Oni with red skin and horns, wearing a strange suit that lit up with captured lightning every time he moved, shook his head.

"It's not boring, jack-ass, it's a period thing, from the American civil war."

Bel nodded his confirmation.

"Yeah, I don't know why you would wear that, but I remember those days. We were really just getting steam up but hadn't figured out how to kill the fucking Watchers yet. We lost a lot of good Sheydim in that battle."

"Less than you might think," Bel answered thoughtfully. He didn't want to deal with these younger creatures anymore, not on an empty stomach. He turned his eyes back to the cook behind the stall. He didn't know what to order, so he turned back towards the three of them. "What is good here, to eat?"

The three of them looked at him like he was an

idiot. Who didn't know what kind of hot dog they liked? Hot dogs were not rocket science; bun, meat, toppings, easy as could be. Finally, the succubus bounced off her perch on the window sill and approached him. His body tensed, his first instinct to crush her body and tear the meat from her bones with his teeth—a relic from a war so long over as to be lost to time. Succubi, the descendants of Lillith, could be so dangerous. They pulled on lust, on longing, on loneliness, and Bel had plenty of all three. Did she sense that? Did she feel like he could be an easy mark, an easy meal? He shifted under his skin, his true self struggling to stay contained. Dara seemed oblivious.

"Well," she said, wrapping her arms around one of his, heedless of the dirt and blood. "I like Chicago style, personally, but JoJo likes his spicy so he gets the sriracha one. Or if you want something sweet like Bohrm, you can get the one with candied bacon." She said all of this clinging to his arm while pointing out various items on the menu.

Bel swallowed his unease. He could feel the slight form of the woman pressing into his arm. Her softness, her hardness. It been so long since he had enjoyed the physical pleasures offered by another living being. Wrenching his attention away from the feel of her body through this sleeve, he nodded and ordered the Chicago style hot dog, as Dara had suggested, and stood uneasily waiting for his food, wondering when the succubus would release him.

"So … has it been a while?" Dara asked, looking up at him. She seemed blind to the grime, blood, filth. Was she asking if he needed a release? "Since you've been topside?" she finished.

"Topside?" Bel rumbled, blinking, thrown off by the sudden change in the direction of his thoughts. "You mean with humans?"

"Yeah, with humans."

"Yes, it has been a while."

"How long?"

Bel was about to snap at her, tell her to mind her damn business and get off his arm, but what was the point in that? Despite his outward nonchalance and his inward turmoil, he was loathe to break contact. Instead, he shrugged.

"It depends on what year it is currently. By my reckoning, my last time was 5626."

"Oh." Her eyes went wide at the realization of how old he must be, and then she smiled, revealing dimples and smile lines. He wondered how much of her kindness and happiness was an act; he wondered what she wanted. "Well, then you have been gone for far too long. Look, you should go back up there, have hot dogs, oh my god, you need to have American pizza, and hamburgers. Like, yes, we have them here, but humans have this, like, unlimited creativity for food that is—" She stopped talking for a moment, withering under his stoic and brutal gaze. She blushed before sheepishly admitting: "I love food."

Bel decided that maybe he liked Dara after all. As she spoke, the press of her body was less alluring, more comfortable. It might simply have been her nature. As her attention went from her metaphysical hunger to the things she actually took pleasure in, her hold on him lessened. Or maybe he was projecting his own thoughts and needs onto her, his attempt to escape the realization of his physical and mental weaknesses after such a long sleep. He reached out with the arm she was clinging to, finally dislodging her in order to take his food.

"Thank you," he offered as he turned to continue his trek, food in hand.

"You're welcome, but if you want to be polite, you could tell me your name, you know, out of politeness ..." Dara watched him, her eyes hungry, though for the hot dog, information, or something more primal, Bel didn't know.

"Bel," he said, seeing no reason to lie.

Bohrm paused, stepping up beside Dara. "Bel? As in the *dragon*?" He looked at Bel, incredulity written across his face, before he glanced at JoJo and Dara, who were staring at him in confusion. "Oh my god, you guys don't remember? Bel was a general, one of the last dragons who died one hundred and fifty years ago fighting one of the Watchers in hand-to-hand combat! He's got a big statue in the …" He paused, realizing, perhaps, that he was gushing about war history no one really cared about but him. "Anyway, your costume makes sense now, a little tacky, though."

Bel didn't answer. The little demon assumed he was wearing a costume and going by a name of a long dead hero. That was almost flattering. He wasn't forgotten, he was immortalized in Sheydim history. The little satyr was staring at him too, though he seemed to see past the glamour and the grime. He was likely older than his two friends; he had seen more, understood more. His mouth was set in a hard little line.

"It isn't a costume, is it?" he asked softly, almost too quiet to be heard over the sound of the roaring celebration rocketing through the City.

Bel met his gaze for a moment, not answering. Behind him, in the light of the fireworks, for a brief second, his shadow took on the form of the massive and terrifying creature he truly was. Bohrm, arguing with Dara over how rude his statement was, missed it. But the little goatman took a step back, unsure how to react to the knowledge of the monster that stood before him, calmly eating a hot dog.

"My friends are assholes, Bel," Dara said when she finally looked up, unaware of anything that had gone on between the man and JoJo. "But they aren't, like, bad assholes. If you want, you can hang out with us tonight, if you don't have other plans." There was an invitation in her words, one that extended past hanging out, possibly past the night and into the morning.

JoJo looked almost panicked at the idea, and Bohrm rolled his eye.

Bel smiled, tempted but driven towards his goal.

"Thank you, no. I have to get to the palace." He raised the rest of his hot dog in a salute of approval before continuing on his path, leaving the confused trio behind; their bickering, teasing, and laughter already fading into the background noise of the City.

The rest of the City was much the same, mixed groups of supernatural creatures in various states of celebration, undress, and rambunctiousness. Down one street Bel had stumbled into, a massive one-eyed Oni squared against a toothsome ogre while a crowd of smaller being pressed in around, shouting bets and egging on the combatants. The chaos of the City was intact, though it seemed that refugees from the world over had found their way to the City East-of-Nod. Bel ignored that for now. He was a solitary creature for the most part. Though the demons surprised him, it didn't concern him. If the Prince and Lillith still ruled over the City, then there would be ample reason behind these decisions. If not, they no longer did …

Bel shook his head; it didn't bear thinking about. By his own reckoning, the night was almost over. He had walked from one end of the City towards the center for several hours, tireless in his path. Soon the artificial sun, a magic that allowed for the light of day to grace the citizens of the City, would rise and paint the buildings in colors as garish as the stone sky above them was gray. For now, though, the palace loomed before him in the darkness of the night.

He paused as he came to the gates, spellwork and guards protected this place. There had been a time when he could come and go as he pleased, but whether or not he would be recognized now, centuries later, was anyone's guess. Just outside the gates, Bel was surprised to find a courtyard filled with rows of statues, each of one of his brothers or sisters. More than Sheydim, these were mythical dragons, Sheydim of immense power, near demigods in their own right.

Bel walked the first row, his haste to reach the palace forgotten for a moment as he remembered the early days. They had been separated from so much of the strife of the early war. Each creature had taken its own dominion and ruled in peace. But in solitude, they had been hunted down, trapped, and slaughtered by the poisoned offspring of Grigori philosophy. Human knights and "heroes" and all manner of hunter had found the dragons and ended them. As strong as they had been, the fallen angels had been stronger, the Nephilim had been more savage. The few that had survived had died later, in the long war against the Grigori. All of them, to a one, himself included; and there, near the middle of the parade of statues, he found himself.

The statue was cast in metal and stood regal and proud. The Sheydim were so resilient, but a war against the monstrous had thinned their numbers. This, Bel realized, was the reason the demons and the refugees had fled to the City East-of-Nod. Without the influx of the demons, the City would be empty; without the addition of other spirits from around the world, the City would die. A Sheyd could not produce more Sheydim, only the Creator's mistakes could do that. When a Sheyd fell with child, it was because of a union with some other creature, and the offspring would either be the other parent's race or, more likely, a demon. And so the uniqueness of the Sheydim was protected, but the longevity of the race was not; and as the dragons had fallen, there could be no replacing them. He noticed a small plaque at the base of his statue.

Bel - Stood Toe to Toe against the Evil of Yeqon, Buying Time For Victory - 5626

It was a memorial tribute … to him.

II

Bel stared up at the statue for a long time, taking in each perfection and chip in the stone. Around it, hundreds more statues stood. He wandered this courtyard of statues, reading each plaque under each statue. Each death struck him like a blow. Some he had known about; Hell, some he had avenged personally. Others he had hoped had survived. But this—he looked over the courtyard of statues—this was genocide, extinction. Every single one of his brothers and sisters, created in the first days of reality, had a statue here, and each one included a date and cause of death. His entire species had been wiped out in a war to protect a humanity that didn't care if they won or lost. All dead now. And for what?

Four, the girl had said, four Grigori banished out of hundreds.

He turned his eyes to the palace. This garden of metal monuments to the death of his people was hollow reward considering the cost. He would get answers, he would understand what happened. He approached the gates finally, ignoring all other revelries within the courtyard. The guards at the gates watched him, slowly coming to attention and waiting for him to get close enough. They wore cloth uniforms, though it seemed they wore plates of hardened leather over the stitched linen. Bel assumed the plates were harder than they appeared, perhaps magical in nature. They had traditional weapons on hand but also wore belts covered in gadgets that reminded Bel of explosives used by humans in various wars, restraints, and what for all the world looked like some form of small rifle. Technology had not stood still while he slept the sleep of the dead.

"No more audiences tonight, my friend," said the shorter of the two guards, a Sheyd with dark complexion and gorgeous green eyes.

When Bel did not slow his pace, the taller of the two, some half giant, it seemed, growled low in warning and reached for a pike. The threat was clear. The gorgeous man didn't reach for his sword, instead opting to place his hand on the firearm at his side. Two threats. Bel didn't know if he was up to a fight after sleeping so long. He didn't know that these two weren't more powerful than he was at the moment. He slowed to a stop.

"They will grant me audience," he rumbled in a growl that put the giant to shame.

The smaller guard shook his head, his smile didn't leave his mouth but had fled from his eyes.

"Perhaps tomorrow, during the day, during more reasonable hours."

"Now," Bel corrected.

"Sir, please turn around, enjoy your night. Tomorrow I will personally deliver your message to the palace."

Bel liked this one, he was formal, attempting diplomacy, and he had chosen looks that were distracting. A clever choice that would have worked if Bel had been less insistent or younger. But Bel saw beauty as a trap. Too many of his kind and too many times he had fallen into a trap for a beautiful man or woman only to wake pinned to a bed with a supposedly magic sword.

"You will not because I will deliver my message myself, and," he took a single step towards them, "I will deliver it tonight." Bel darted forward, his legs carrying him with a speed neither of the guards were expecting.

For all that, they reacted admirably, moving their weapons to block his passage.

Bel planted a foot between the smaller guard's legs, one arm gripping the man's neck while the other grabbed his waist. He twisted and pulled, flinging the smaller guard over his hip in one smooth motion, ripping the gun out of its holster as he did so. He didn't watch the guard's rag doll tumble through the air, already moving to deal with the other. He was faster than he looked.

The giant's weapon crashed into the ground, shaking the earth as Bel stepped aside. Bel lifted the gun and attempted to fire into the mass of the larger guard, and was only rewarded with hollow clicks but no shot fired. Cursing, Bel cast the gun aside; he didn't have time to figure out how it worked as the giant was already lifting his pike for a second swing. Bel charged the giant, his own talon-tipped fingers swiping at the leather plates stretched across the guard. He did not penetrate the armor but felt the power of magical wards woven into the fabric and hardened plates. His attack had left him open, and the giant took advantage.

The terrible impact from the haft of the pike was enough to send Bel stumbling a dozen feet back. His arm stung and hung at his side, numb and unresponsive for a moment before the pain bloomed out. He could deal with pain, he could fight through pain. He was about to charge back into the fight with the giant when something sharp skewered him from behind. Looking down, he saw a sword, the sword that the smaller guard had had by his side. It protruded sideways from his stomach before wrenching out carrying guts, bile, and fluid with it. Bel sank to one knee, his hands clutching at his intestines, forcing them back in, trying to hold the wound shut.

The smaller guard, the one who had struck the blow, moved to stand in front of Bel, a smirk on his face. "It looks like your message won't be delivered after all." He wiped the viscera off his sword on Bel's shoulder.

"Impudent," Bel whispered.

"Sorry, what was that?" The smug Sheyd leaned forward to hear better. "I can't hear you over the sound of your—"

Whatever else he was going to say was lost as Bel's jaw unhinged and a gout of searing hot fiery phlegm burst forward and engulfed the Sheyd's head. He screamed, falling backwards, but the phlegm clung to the flesh, spreading wherever he clawed at his flesh trying to put out the flames. Bel stood, still holding his side, watching the conflagration as the man's eyes burst from the heat and his skin melted like wax, running in rivulets of boiling blood and fat over the front of his uniform. Bel raised his orange eyes, glowing beside the fire, to the giant. The screams stopped; only the pop and hiss of the man's remains boiling away to ash remained.

The giant considered for a moment, unsure how to respond to the death of his partner. Bel regretted the death, there appeared to be too few Sheydim left, but he would not be questioned or barred entry, not by Sheyd, Demon, or Dybbuk.

"Go, raise alarm, do what you will, but if you come at me or bar my path again, I will end more than this life tonight." He took a step towards the giant, lifting the arm that had been holding his stomach together. The wound had sealed shut, though bits of torn flesh still hung and blood still coated his hips and waist. The giant wisely chose to turn tail and run. Bel relaxed his arms. That had taken a lot out of him, more than it should. He would need to eat more, and to rest, to retrain his body into the weapon it had once been. But for now, he could enter the palace and demand answers as to why his kind's lives had been thrown away so cheaply.

It took very little time for the guards to react. They emerged from doors and barracks, swarming like a tide of ravenous ants to surround Bel. He paid them no mind. He strode forward, approaching the front door of the palace. The ring of guards kept their distance, an ever-moving circle of inward pointed spears and pikes. No one was brave enough to come at him first; none of them recognized him.

When they reached the massive door leading into the palace, Bel stopped. He turned in a tight circle, taking in the arms and guards arrayed against him. Could he take them all? On his best day, easily. But this was not his best day; he had already been wounded, and he could only force his body to heal so much damage at once. He turned back towards the doors of the palace. Would this then be his last stand? Would he have slumbered through centuries of healing only to be torn apart by his own in the doorway of a palace he had served? Would they recognize him as they carried his corpse past his own statue?

"Stop!" The command was sharp and sudden, a voice that had all the power of an immovable object.

Bel craned his neck to see over the guards to where the voice came from. He was prepared to be the unstoppable force that crashed against any who defied him. The sea of guards parted for their Moses who strode forth, a fierce woman whose words spilled from her mouth without pause.

"I do not know who you are to attack the palace, but know that I will not sacrifice any of my guards for your benefit. You've taken one life, and for that you will pay with your … Bel?" The woman who had stomped her way to stand before him, bellowing the entire time, came to a sudden stop in front of Bel. This guard was no young blood. She had an old and grizzle air. She was known.

"Hello, Agrat bat Mahlat. I've come to speak to your grandparents."

Agrat, the granddaughter of Lillith, a powerful force of magic and strength, a seducer in her youth and a commander of armies in her maturity, was taken aback by the sight of Bel. She had not expected any disturbances tonight, let alone for Bel, dead Bel, to be at the center of them. She looked around at the ocean of faces around them. How could she save face? If she tried to detain Bel, he would kill, maybe her, maybe not, but people would certainly die, and what would her grandmother say? On the other hand, she had to save face, she had to take charge, or else these demons and spirits would never listen to her. Control and order in the City East-of-Nod existed on a knife's edge, and the sudden appearance of Bel could certainly throw that off.

"Bel ..." He was as handsome as ever, though she could hardly tell under all the grime and gore. She almost smiled. He was the serpent, not the proverbial one, though he might as well have been. She watched his face with quizzical purple eyes before turning away from him. Showing her back to an attacker would be a death sentence, but she doubted she had anything to fear from Bel if she didn't antagonize him. "Back to your barracks and stations, leave Bel to me."

There were murmurs, strangled gasps, and other noise from the guards. They were concerned about abandoning their commander. Some who knew the name were disturbed at what that could mean, while others merely kvetched about having been woken up so close to morning. But they went, dispersing from the courtyard in sullen waves until the dragon and the demoness were alone.

"You look like shit."

"First words a friend says to me in centuries, and they are *you look like shit*. Hardly seems fair," Bel returned, not moving for a moment before he allowed himself to deflate. No need to look powerful in front of Agrat. She knew who and what he was, there was no sense in puffing up.

"They may not be fair, but the words are true …" She had a thousand questions for him, ten thousand! Where had he been? How was he alive? Why come back now? Did he remember what happened? Did he know what had happened since? But the only one she asked for now was: "Could you really not wait until morning? I remember you being more patient than that."

Bel's molten orange eyes, burning with an internal light, shone bright in the shadow of the palace as he regarded the woman before him. He stood like his statue—stoic, strong, and silent. Agrat moved forward and briefly hugged him. The sudden affection caught him off guard, but he was not surprised. The Sheydim were not a cloistered lot afraid of their own emotions and actions like humans were. He rubbed her back briefly through the strange armor before stepping back to look more closely. The armor was not the form fitting affair that succubi often fought in, nor the platemail that he remembered serious warriors donning; it looked more like his current union uniform than armor.

"I think I like this new armor. It looks easier to move in than that you used to wear to war."

She looked down at herself and nodded. She took his arm, much the same way the succubus earlier had, and began leading him into the palace. "It is. We call it tactical body armor. It was initially designed by humans to fight in their wars. It stops bullets for the most part, slicing weapons are almost worthless against it. And of course, we use magic to strengthen the protection it offers. You know you will be waking them at this hour?"

"Agrat," Bel begged, "surely I have waited long enough. I can be forgiven haste now, the City is a different creature now. I have no clothes, no possessions at all, and what I want to know is so simple …"

"What is it you want to know?"

"Why am I alive? Why are the rest of my kind dead?"

Agrat stopped walking and turned to face Bel. "I'm afraid you'll not find satisfying answers here Bel, but … I know the prince will give his best answers." She looked around the empty throne room in which they had stopped and nodded to herself, making a decision. "Wait here, I'll go get them."

The throne room was massive, large enough for the court of the Sheydim to gather in great numbers and the people of the City to come before their royalty to make demands, amends, or the case for help from the palace. It was also nearly bare of ornamentation. Though the Sheydim could be a gaudy lot when the mood struck them, the prince had disdained to create a show of wealth here. It looked more like the halls of a humble monastery than the seat of power for a kingdom nearly as old as creation.

Bel stood as still and silent as a snake regarding prey. His eyes moved across the thrones and the stonework of the great hall, the only movement that betrayed life within the statuesque stance the dragon took. It was several minutes before anyone reentered the hall. A messenger entered; it looked human, which was not entirely surprising, but this one smelled human. Bel didn't react or move to meet the man, letting him come all the way to him. Bel realized that this man was essentially human, just not living. A dybbuk gifted with physical form by the court.

The spirit reached him and lifted a hand to

signify he would speak as soon as he caught his breath. "Sorry." He finally gulped. "No cell service down here." He grinned as though he was being terribly clever, but Bel had no idea what the hell he was talking about. Getting no reaction for his joke, the ghost sighed and straightened up to deliver his message. "King Ashmandai Ben Ayin and Queen Lilit bat HaShem request the …" the spirit paused as if he were confused by the wording he had been given. "The honor of your company. If you would follow me."

Bel wondered where Agrat had gone but followed the ghost through the halls of the palace. Though he kept his neck straight, his eyes roamed over every detail, seeking to find what had changed and what had remained the same during his long slumber. Once they passed through the throne room, the palace began looking the part. Rich tapestries hung everywhere, telling the stories of thousands of battles, struggles, and triumphs throughout history. He was surprised to see that not only had so much more been added but, again, it seemed inclusion reigned even within the palace, with demons being given equal honor to the Sheydim natives.

The Dybbuk led Bel through the winding passages, through halls and past rooms designed for war, armories, dojos, and libraries. The palace was not empty either. Every room Bel looked in was occupied. People stood engaged in study or conversation, contemplation or action. It felt more like a community center than a palace at the moment, another change, one that Bel was ill at ease with. He had always been a solitary creature, even when he had spent time within the City, he had his own home. His own home ... Bel wondered idly if he still had a home. If the caverns he had once occupied had been emptied out, his horde plundered, his memories defaced. That would be his second stop.

The dybbuk finally stopped and stepped to one side of a door, allowing Bel entry into another room. By his own estimation, they were deep in the depths of the palace. He could feel the dampness in the air and smell the underground springs.

Indeed, as he stepped into the room, he discovered a subterranean cavern and hot spring. Behind him, the door swung closed. The cavern was lit with sparsely placed braziers, whose flickering light flung shadows all over the room and caused strange refractions of light to dance across every surface. Bel waited for his eyes to adjust but finally found them. Lillith sat near the back; her body, bereft of any dressing, was the epitome of human women. She was lust, she was love, nurturing and defiant. Mothering and wild, passion and reason, empathy and cruelty all wrapped in the flawless skin of the first woman. The blackness of her skin was an inky darkness on the backdrop of night. The whites of her eyes widened as they met with his.

"I had hoped but was afraid it was not true." Lillith's voice held the same mystique as her body. It pulled at the part of him that was male and craved sex. It pulled at the part of him that needed a mother, needed to be comforted. It pulled at the part of him that craved a friend. Bel wondered how any resisted her, then remembered that most could not, least of all mortal men.

"I never doubted. I knew you had survived. Death, impossible." This voice came from the shadows themselves, and the speech pattern was unmistakable. Ashmandai was visible only in the reddish eyes that separated from the rest of the shadows before taking a more solid shape. While Lillith was a human woman, perhaps the most human, the most woman to ever exist, Ashmandai was no such thing. He was Bel's brother in creation, more than most other Sheydim, though less than the other dragons. Ashmandai was a beautiful man, he was as perfect as an unfinished thing could be. Physically, he took a shape that would be pleasing to his queen, though shape meant so little to the half-finished Sheydim.

Bel clasped his hands behind his back, forcing himself to not kneel or bow before them. He was too powerful and too proud to do so.

"Hush. Ash, I don't know who you're putting on a show for," Lillith chided her husband before rising and moving towards Bel. Every movement of her nude form cast new shadows and new reflections throughout the room. Each step shifted her hips in a hypnotic tick-tock, a rhythm that was near impossible to ignore, the muscles in her legs and abdomen shifting just under the skin as she approached. Bel didn't move, even when the Queen of the Sheydim wrapped her arms around him and rested her head against his chest. "We missed you, old friend, but …" she stepped back, looking over him. "You are filthy and you smell." From lover to mother, Lillith shifted seamlessly between roles, open and honest with her nature and herself in a way so few in any realm could be.

"I wear the clothes I died in," Bel stated softly, irritated at how embarrassed he was to be so unkempt in her presence. He had raged in his mind, planning sharp words and rage towards the rulers of the city, but now, as Lillith pulled on his buttons, undressing him before her husband, he felt like a child who was caught stealing cookies. Lillith was one of the few beings in all of creation older than he was. "I came straight here upon awakening."

"I understand." Lillith paused in her undressing to cup his cheek tenderly, then went back to her task. "I'll send for new clothes. Fashion has changed since you last walked among us, you'll stand out more than usual with these. And by the Creator, Bel, shed this look, this skin ..."

Fully nude now, as naked as Lillith and Ashmandai, Bel moved to the water, staring down at his dim reflection in the low lights. He was bloody and barely recognized the face he had died in. It was an old face, worn by a war fought between brothers, with gray hairs streaking through the blond in both the scalp and the beard. The beard itself was wild, an expansion of what had once been a well kept mustache and goatee. It was an alien face, worn to get close to Yeqon in the days of the American Civil War. It was useless now, or at least, *for* now. He shed it, shaking himself like a dog whipping away water after a bath. The illusion fell away and dissipated like smoke in a breeze. Left behind was the dark caramel skin he had adopted as his first human look. Though his golden-orange eyes remained, they shifted in shape, becoming like almonds and slit like a crocodile's. He grew as well, bulkier, more muscle, longer limbs and fingers. His nails, cracked and broken, hardened and lengthened into short talons. The scars he had taken from other immortal beings through the ages remained—cuts here, claws there, ragged teeth marks in some places. He could still pass as human, so long as no one looked too closely, but this was as close to a true form as he had without taking the form of a great and terrible wyrm.

He felt Lillith's hands on his back. "That is so much better now." She pushed him gently, guiding him into the water. "Clean off the blood and dirt and grime."

Once he was in the water, Ashmandai approached, watching as his wife ran her hands over Bel's body, rinsing away the dirt and blood. There was no jealousy, no distrust, no possessiveness in his eyes as he stood there waiting. Finally, he spoke.

"I am sorry, Bel. It took a very long time. The angel took you."

"Took me?"

"Yes." Lillith whispered. "We thought at first he had killed you, but we never found your body; and we searched, believe me, Bel, we searched with every means at our disposal. But he had taken you and hidden you." She paused, her hands on his lower abdomen as though asking permission to continue cleaning. Nothing was forbidden in the City, but everything was consensual.

Bel gave a slight nod, unwilling—or maybe

unable—to end the contact.

"Yeqon had designs, a torturous plan for you, for eternity," Ashmandai explained quietly, his powerful arms crossed over his chest. From the beginning, Ashmandai spoke in this rhythm, creating haiku of conversation before Nippon had even existed. Bel doubted the prince could even speak any other way.

Bel turned his eyes to Lillith as her nails trailed against his body, which ached in need. She didn't fondle or grope, merely cleaned. She made no comment over his hardness and neither took notice of the way his breath staggered whenever her hands cleaned in sensitive places. After too long—and too short—a time, she reached up with water cupped in her hands to wash the blood and grime off his face. When she finished, she gave him a sweet smile and stepped back.

"Do you feel better now?" she asked.

He took a moment to consider her; she was as multi-faceted a creature that ever existed, capable of the kindest gestures and the most terrible rages. In truth, this kindness, this gentleness was a rare glimpse into the personality of the Succubus Queen that few other than the inner circle of closest friends ever saw.

"Later," she said, "I can find someone willing to help with your ... tension."

"I'm fine. I do not need you to *find* someone for me." He was too proud to allow his queen to play matchmaker, even for something as simple as a fling. And he did feel better, at least physically. His old skin, bereft of the centuries old grime, was a welcome change almost forgotten. "But I walked the courtyard of statues, and I would have an explanation."

"What explanation, could there be for what happened? Draconic warfare," Ashmandai stated simply.

Bel turned his eyes to Lillith for a more nuanced statement. For her part, she walked back to her husband's side and took his hand in hers.

"After your fall," Ashmandai said, "most of your kind demanded justice. They went berserk at the thought that Yeqon held you captive. They stormed our palace, and who among the Sheydim could stop them other than us? So they gained entry and then demanded that they be allowed to make open war against the Grigori … to retrieve your body."

"I was dead, why would they care?"

"You were not dead, Bel! You were captured and hidden, kept a prisoner," Ashmandai said exasperated.

"I never died?"

"You didn't, Bel." Lillith continued. "I think

Yeqon knew that if you were dead, your strength would return to the other dragons, and so you were kept alive and tortured, your body too traumatized to recover enough to wake but never enough to kill you. Your siblings led the final fight against Yeqon in Libya roughly a decade ago. It was bloody, it was ruthless, and those that had not died in other wars were killed there." Lillith fell silent, the pain of that day etched on her face just over the raging storm of hatred and anger. Bel could see her body trembling with force of effort to not fly to the world above and rip angels feather from flesh until naught was left but bones.

"The dragons attacked, before we were prepared, before he was weak." The prince moved to the edge of the pool, pulling himself out of the water and grabbing a robe, which he draped around his body in soft folded cloth. "But they cleared the way, weakened his hold on humans, his power folded."

"We learned, during the second world war ..." She paused, realizing that Bel would have no way of knowing what that meant. "We learned during one of the worst wars we had seen that to truly end their threat, to make them weak enough to return to a kind of Sheol, we had to first dismantle their power. We had to rip apart the infrastructure around them. Yeqon ruled Libya as Muammar, and when your siblings murdered his attending angels, and as the humans were incited to rebel, Yeqon became exposed and vulnerable."

"A gift of his head, delivered to Semyaza, in person, by me." Ashmandai moved to the door and called for clothes to be brought for Bel.

"And we were able to find your body, and bring you here to heal, though it had taken so long, we feared you would never awaken."

"I ..." Bel moved to the edge of the pool and sat heavily on the edge. He was the last then, and he had no one to blame but the dead. There was no vengeance, no raging justice he could visit on anyone. He closed his eyes. He was tired, so tired. His kind hadn't died uselessly to win a war, his kind had died uselessly for him. Because he had fought in a war. "I was told you've dealt with four of them."

"Azazel, Yeqon, B'ruchiel, and Shedza, they each fell to us." Ashmandai counted them off on his six fingered hand.

"Then the war continues?" Bel asked.

Ashmandai watched the last dragon carefully before nodding.

III.

"Then my part is not done either." Bel growled, enraged that he had slumbered while the Watchers had slaughtered his kind. He was decided. He rose from the edge of the pool and exited, leaving the two alone in the soothing waters of the hot spring. "I will return to the surface to join battle." He paused to take the bundle of clothes that was offered him by a maid, who exited as silently as she had entered. Dressing quickly, he stood looking at the royalty of the City, waiting for them to argue with him.

Lillith wordlessly sighed, seeming to almost resent leaving the water. All were silent, drinking in the vision of Lillith emerging from the pool, putting shame to Venus with her beauty and divinity.

"Are you sure that is what you want, Bel?" Lillith asked. "You have more than earned respite. Not something I ever offered my husband, but you, you may rest."

"His mind is now set. He seeks to bring death to them, perhaps we can help," Ashmandai offered to his wife, but the wheels were turning behind the ancient Sheyd's eyes. He had a plan to take advantage of Bel's rage and power. "You cannot face them toe-to-toe or face-to-face, you must besiege them." Ashmandai left the room, walking through the halls of the palace and trusting his friend and wife to follow.

"You have a plan," Bel stated, not questioning. Ashmandai always did. He took the long view of all things, perhaps more so than almost any other creature in existence. "Will you share it?"

"We learned during war, that by destabilizing, they could be made weak." Ashmandai paused, though if he were thinking or if it were merely the unnatural rhythm of his speech was anyone's guess. He turned and continued down a new hallway. "With this in mind, Bel, we can formulate a plan where you can crush them."

"My husband hopes to guide the blade that will severe Semyaza's head." Lillith walked beside Bel and behind Ashmandai. She reached over and took his hand as she spoke, the easy affection of the first woman completely natural, impossible to be unwelcome. "You cannot do this alone, or, I fear, at all. The methods of war and the needs of secrecy are profound and profoundly different than they used to be."

"None will keep me from this war, Lillith, not even you. I will return to the surface."

"Fighting there would be, detrimental to us all, but there are other ways," Ashmandai offered.

"You mean to send Bel to the islands?" Lillith

came to a halt, bringing their small entourage to a stop.

"I think them perfect, for a warrior such as Bel, no need to constrain." Ashmandai explained all of this to Lillith patiently.

Lillith, for her part, nodded thoughtfully, seeing her husband's logic.

"To the islands then, at least for now, a training grounds of sort." She resumed her movement down the hall, dragging Bel with her, while Ashmandai fell behind with a wry grin.

After a few moments, Ashmandai stepped around the two and opened a door for Bel. "This will serve for now, a room and abode for you, until you return to war."

The room he had led them to was an opulent den of obsidian. Red velvet banners hung from the ceiling, and furniture of black glass had been carved into the walls. A cursory glance revealed that many of his belongings, treasures hoarded through long centuries, had been relocated here. They had set so much in motion circling around his eventual return. Bel stepped into the room and looked around. He was satisfied, understanding that this meant the home he had left behind was gone. This would do.

"Tomorrow, we'll meet with Agrat and Uhstiel, we will find you a place to best bring your vengeance and prepare you for the modern world, as well as the strange war that exists on the islands." Lillith said all of this with a grin; she couldn't entirely hide the vicious smile at the thought of killing more of the repugnant fallen angels. "It is good to have you back, Bel." And with that, the royal family of the City East-of-Nod left him to his own devices.

But Bel did not sleep.

He had slept for centuries, undreaming, dead for all intent and purposes. Rescued from an eternity of torture by his now dead siblings. He spent the rest of the evening exploring his new home, seeing what knick-knacks and relics had been rescued from his old hoard and brought here. A part of him panicked for each bauble that was missing. He pushed the feeling deep down into his gut to fester. He was a hoarder, a collector of things, and his things were gone. He ran his talons over ancient swords taken from would-be knights, and skulls inlaid with gold and gems that he had ripped from lesser angels during the great war. Trophies of battles, books he would never read, art that would never be seen by mankind because he had stolen it from the homes of incredible artists before they could sell or show it. This room held a hundredth of what he had collected over the long centuries.

A part of him recognized that these things were the things of worth, the best and most intact specimens from his hoard—he had never been discerning. This collection was organized. It was laid out and easy to admire. There were large leather folios filled with art and designs he had taken from Michelangelo's workshop, and swords crafted by the greatest mortal sword smiths to ever live. But it was not everything. The loss hurt deep as a wound, and he considered directing his rage back at Ashmandai. After all, who else would have overseen the transfer of his hoard? Who else would have given his home away to some other … lesser Sheyd? For hours, the dragon considered and perused his withered hoard, long past the hours of night and into the strange artificial dawn that was unique to the City East-of-Nod.

Bel sat on the edge of the bed. He considered losing himself to a rage, smashing these things that Ashmandai had salvaged. Why not lose everything? Why not give up everything? Rationally, he realized that the majority of those things lost were shreds and broken remnants of a life left behind. But there were things in his hoard, things now missing, that had been given to him by siblings. Now with them gone, he would have sought comfort in the material objects they had left behind. He was denied even this. Throughout his black glass chambers were the remains of history. Within this room were the bones of creation from the first few moments until … until roughly 200 years ago.

He would need to rectify that. He had last left the world of the living during an age of gunpowder and exploration. When all people hated all other people. The fledgling country of America had been in the throes of tearing itself apart then, and the warlords of Europe, locked in an endless cycle of expansion under the cruel guidance of the Grigori. What had changed? What new ways of killing and pain had humans invented since he had last walked their world?

It wasn't all bad; the hot dog had been delicious. And assuming the fashion of the City East-of-Nod had kept up with the world above, things had come a long way from the rough wools and leathers he had left behind. He moved to a mirror and gazed at the clothes draped over his body. They were simple robes, soft and supple, black with golden thread weaving designs that seemed alive with fire and movement. These were traditional, what he would have worn thousands of years ago, but what he had seen from the people in the streets were different. Not robes but form fitting cloth, which seemed designed to accent the shape of the body more than anything else. He wrinkled his nose at the colors of the robes. Black was never his color when in human form. He preferred creams and whites, clothes that would contrast the darkness of his skin tones, making him look darker, more stark, more powerful.

His thoughts were interrupted by a sudden presence in his room. He glanced over his shoulder in the mirror and saw a man, short, powerfully built. His skin was magma that rolled with fury within his own dark robes, his hair was flame, and he looked for all the world like the birth of a tiny star. But Bel recognized this particular Djinn. This corrupted piece of divinity-infused human.

"Kolu-bechal"

"Lord Bel."

They stood in silence for many moments, not speaking, the tension heavy in the air. Bel had never trusted the Djinn, demons born of Nephilim's cruelty. These were the offspring of the offspring of the enemy. Why Ashmandai had spared them even as he orchestrated the downfall of the Nephilim, Bel could not say.

Finally, the Djinn shook out his fiery mane and stepped back, gesturing to the door.

"You're called to breakfast. Lord Bel."

The icy resentment within the Djinn set Bel's teeth on edge, and he longed to rip his throat out for his insolence. Was it Kolu's grandfather who had tortured him for centuries? Was it his uncle who had murdered Bel's kin? His resentment was no mystery. Bel had argued loud and long against the inclusion of the Djinn in the City East-of-Nod. He considered killing Kolu where he stood. He was not Sheydim, and Bel would not mourn his death, but it would be the second murder he committed in as many days, and Bel knew that soon the blood would flow freely.

Wordlessly, he followed the Djinn back through the palace.

After a lavish breakfast of fruits, pastries, and delicacies, most of which Bel had never tried before, Ashmandai left them to attend to the business of running an empire. Agrat watched as dishes and platters were removed, and when all was clear, she unfurled a large map of the world over the table. It was covered in marks and notes, things circled and crossed off. Various countries were lined in red. This, Bel realized, was a battle map, but on a grander scale than anything he had seen before. There were no front lines, the battles were fought over territory that, according to the map, had changed hands multiple times throughout the long years.

Here in the City, things were handled succinctly. Word was taken at face value among beings that had existed so long that the status quo seemed immutable. He had stated his intent to return to the ancient war, he would do so. His prince and queen wasted no time in fulfilling his wish.

"This is the human world, as they know it, the battlegrounds. We sow coups and dissent from the established rule of the Watchers. We call it the War of Dictates because we use political sway, rules, and public opinion to weaken the hold of the Grigori before we strike them down. It is slow, and it is a different kind of war, it is one of subtlety that the angels seem incapable of."

Agrat smiled up at Bel with a warmth she rarely showed others. Bel was charming and handsome when he wanted to be, but any demon or Sheydim could manage that. Bel was strong, stoic, and driven, all traits she admired. She had studied war under him, during the conflict against the demons. Serving her grandparents against her own kind. To now be planning decisive strikes against angelic filth beside a hero like him was an honor. Bel met her smile with the barest upturn of his lips. Kindness and warmth did not come naturally to him, even when he was around those he considered his family.

"As I'm sure grandfather has told you, we have dealt with Yeqon and with Azazel, two great powers who had overstretched themselves considerably."

"He mentioned them, yes." Bel looked down at the map, tracing a lazy talon along the Mississippi River in the northern American continent, where he had *died*. "Has Azazel's exit from the war resulted in less ..." he gestured aimlessly in the air.

"Unfortunately not, Bel," Lillith answered, her face a dark storm of simmering rage at remembering Azazel's violence against her children and the abuse Ashmandai had suffered at his hands. "His gifts to humanity remain in play, and he nearly perfected the art of genocide, a lasting scar of the psyche of humanity that continues to poison them against equity and freedom."

Bel nodded. Azazel had originally gifted the humans with the art of weapons. A violent warmongering monster, he had been the first Grigori that Ashmandai had waged war against, and he had thoroughly destroyed the Sheydim forces whenever they had met in battle, no matter the numbers or tactical advantage.

"The angels remain separated, only gathering in pairs at most, other than their attendant angels or other demonic forces that have sided with them over the long centuries," Agrat said with barely disguised disgust. "My best guess is that if they gathered as they had before the flood, they would attract the attention of Enoch once again. So long as they maintain their own fiefdoms and kingdoms, the Creator and the angels seem content letting the Grigori be our and humanity's problem."

"Not even our old allies?" Bel questioned, wondering what had become of Kamdiel, the angel of justice who seemed to hate the Grigori more than even Lillith, if such a thing were possible.

"Of course, our old allies do what they can, but they are rigid in their ways, Bel. We can't count on them to win this war … they are good for battles, but battles can't kill or even end the threat of the Watchers," Lillith answered softly.

As they spoke, more and more Sheydim joined them around the table—warriors and strategists, it seemed, from the way they mutely observed the map as though waiting for orders.

"So how do we end a Watcher?" Bel finally asked, tired of the mystery behind how they had turned the tables.

Agrat smiled, relishing the thought of battle, of carnage, and of taking the war to the ancient enemy. "We dissolve their support. The Watchers feed off domination. The worship and fear of those beneath them swell their power. As their support crumbles, as the people rebel and their own followers die or mutiny, they become weaker, capable of being torn apart and captured."

"Captured?" Bel asked, intrigued at the

thought. "Are you saying we have a prison with fallen angels as captives?"

"No," Lillith sighed. "Not as such. We capture their essence in a vessel, using the oldest magic my husband could find. We bind them there, and then we turn them over."

"Turn them over? To who? Not Enoch." Bel snarled. "That fool let them loose before and would do so again."

"To their brother, Kamdiel, who, as I understand it, sets guardian angels over the vessels, guarding them from being set loose again," Agrat explained patiently.

"Guerrilla combat, insurrection, infighting, assassination, and civil unrest. These are the tools to topple tyrants on Earth. No matter how much you wish to go and fight the Grigori head-on as you did at your last battle, doing so will end as your last battle did," Lillith said, tracing a slow circle on the map with her finger.

"But that is not the only option, here." Agrat pointed at a portion of the ocean that seemed shrouded in mists, even on the map. "Within these mists exists a separate reality, a different realm. A place where magic, monsters, and mayhem are a daily reality. A few of the Watchers have taken roost here, becoming warlords and enjoying a meager existence in what they believe to be the relative safety out of sight of the Creator and his angels."

"But not safe from us," Bel murmured.

"Not safe from you," Lillith corrected, the smile she wore thoughtful and eager for the spilled blood of divine and wretched creatures.

"These are their lands, and when pressed, they may even drag sections of earth into those misty realms, but there we have no compunction to play nice, no reason to hide power," Agrat finished.

"You will need some training; you will need to understand the danger you are in, those you will work with, and the objectives. Destruction and mayhem will get you far, but working with a small team will allow you to destabilize their entire power base. And then … and then we may begin the good work of ending a life eternal."

Bel had argued he didn't need to be trained on the arts of war and weaponry; he had, after all, fought for centuries. He had encountered cannons and guns and used swords and spells. He had besieged ancient cities and torn down defensive walls. It had taken Ashmandai taking him aside, explaining in no uncertain terms that technology had changed, not just in small bits here and there but suddenly and explosively. That there were things that science and human technology could do that magic had yet to emulate.

Bel had scoffed at first, until Agrat had taken him to the firing range—a training course for her soldiers—and shown him first hand the destructive power of her new toys. Hand held guns that spat metal faster than he could have imagined, at an intense and insane rate. Body armor that could deflect most of these bullets, knives designed to slice and create wounds that would not seal back up. And cars, motorcycles, planes, all manner of machine that could move a massive number of soldiers or civilians about. And that wasn't even looking at the computers. This was the strangest bit to him. The thing he thought was most like the magic he had known. Devices that could communicate with other machines, that could instantly access all the world's information faster than even the Sheyd could travel. In a day and age when computers existed, what use were the magical powers of the demons and Sheydim?

Bel stood in the same body armor that Agrat wore. He was impressed at the lack of ornamentation; there were no signs or outward symbols of leadership, nothing for an assassin to identify him by. Used to either wearing bulky plates of metal or being unprotected, it felt odd to be sent into battle wearing something so lackluster.

Then again, the last war he had fought had been fought in what amounted to pajamas.

"In a war over a hundred and fifty years ago, Uncle!" Agrat said, exasperated. "You have to understand that these are not the same. We are sending you in to start a new war, in a place where you can rend your opponents with claw and tooth and terrible flames. On the islands, magic and melee are still viable options. But we can never know how the Grigori will have prepared. Do not let overconfidence give you the illusion that we are on equal footing."

Bel lowered his eyes a moment, considering her words. It had been a thousand years or more since she'd called him uncle. His family, his fellow dragons all dead, he had no real family. He looked back at the woman who stood before him—proud and strong, a leader of her people. He could take pride in the warrior princess she had become. He looked down at the weapon in his hand—a compact chunk of metal that spat bullets out at a mind-bending rate, without even having to be loaded each time!

"You are saying that it is possible I will not need to use this thing at all?" he finally asked.

"We'll prepare you for any possibility, Bel. Your team will be ready to answer any questions and help with the specifics."

"And where is this team? Should I not meet them?"

"You will. They left this morning in order to scout and prepare the way. Your job is to learn as much as you can about the Islands and about the changes in the world before you join them. Trust me, Bel, we will prepare you for whatever comes."

She had not been lying. Over the next few months, they had impressed upon him that he would need to not just be a fighter and a warrior but a leader; he would need to inspire the supernatural and the human alike. Only then, when their empire crumbled, would a Watcher be weakened enough to dispatch. They explained all the tools, all the gadgets, all of the ins and outs of the plan.

His mornings were spent on obstacle courses and training ranges, going through forms and stances and every manner of combat and self-defense. He sparred, he studied, stoic but impatient. In the evenings, he would regale his fellow trainees with stories of the oldest war, of mistakes Agrat had made as a young warrior, and about the battles of the War of Dictates. He would spin the tales of standing back-to-back with Kamdiel and Prince Ashmandai as they tore through the lesser angels on the plague-ridden plains of Europe. And at night, he would retire alone to his opulent and cold chamber. He could have his pick of partners, he could smell the interest in the men, women, and those that defied easy classifications. And while he caught their glimpses, he ignored them. He was much too interested in finally going to war.

Beyond even the preparation of combat, Lillith pulled him aside in the evenings and lectured him on the history of the world since his death. She spoke of the march of technology, and events in this world and the world of the humans. Facts and dates and oddities filled his skull to nearly breaking. When he felt like he could listen no more, it was finally time.

Ashmandai opened a portal, and Bel stepped through … and found himself 4,000 miles above the southern jungle island ruled by Habbiel.

Jungles of Habbiel

I.

Having stepped through a portal in the City East-of-Nod, Bel, the last dragon, once the champion of the Sheydim and now resurrected from a death-like state, found himself plummeting through the clouds above a small green island shrouded in mist.

Bel opened his orange eyes wide, a secondary transparent lens protecting them from the wind as he shot through the lower atmosphere above the island. Even from his ever-decreasing high altitude, he could make out the complex little towns and cities that dotted the jungle landscape. These would be the battlegrounds; these would be the places he had to sway away from the cruel tyranny of the Watcher that controlled this place with an iron fist. The wind rushing past him created such a roar that he could barely hear his own thoughts. Stretching his arms out, Bel unfurled his wings; great, leathery, and black as a lunar eclipse, they caught the wind. He hung there like a dark jewel in the sky, still too far above the world to be spotted by the population below.

Somewhere down there amongst the natural green and the man-made structures of the world, there were allies. Sheydim who had been infiltrating this country for years, getting in place for the big push. Bel was to be that big push. Flapping lazily, Bel scanned the world beneath him until he spotted the river Agrat had told him about. Along its bend would be his compatriots. He closed his wings tight against his body, allowing them to merge with his being and disappear entirely as he resumed his plummet towards the ground. He angled himself, watching calmly as the ocean of green rushed up to meet him. Elsewhere, people pointed at the sky, trying to identify the huge black bird that had suddenly appeared and was diving towards something in the jungle.

Bel closed his eyes. The rushing air was like the old days, when he could take the form of the mighty wyrm and fly through the air to crush his enemies. The freedom and exhilaration were palpable, they were a flavor on his tongue. He longed to shed the human shape and bask in the sun in his true form. But that would not do, not now, not yet. Instead, he reopened his eyes and twisted his body, angling until he was a black arrow shooting towards the world. He dove into the deep waters of the massive river. Moments later, he surfaced and began swimming towards the shore. Ashmandai had cautioned him to not rely on supernatural powers too much once he was inside the bounds of Habbiel's little feudal country of Ilaat, lest he attract the attention of angels before he was ready for the slaughter. Bel had begun pulling himself out of the water when a hand, soft and small, gripped his forearm and helped tug him out of the river.

"You must be the operative that General Agrat mentioned." The woman who had pulled him out of the river was slight but attractive. She looked like a native of these lands, her dark caramel skin well suited to the sun and jungle heat, though her electric blue hair stood out. She stood in front of him, hands on her tiny waist, grinning up with a huge smile plastered on her face. She had adorable dimples that, despite only having met her once, he immediately recognized.

"Dara," he responded, surprised to find the succubus who had taught him about hot dogs here. And not just Dara, looking over his shoulder, he spotted Jojo and Bohrm. All were in human form but hardly disguising their identities. Dara's smile grew wider.

"Wait! Who are ... do I know you?" She peered up at him and patted his chest and arms as though taking stock. "I think I would remember you," she said, almost to herself.

"Bel. We met ... some time ago, during a celebration," he answered. "I wore the face of a white man dressed in blue."

"Oh ... Wow, I do remember that; you didn't know what a hot dog was!" She smiled wryly up at him. "When I said you needed to come top side, I didn't mean to the islands. I meant to, like, one of the big human cities." She took his hand in hers; he let her—between Agrat and Lillith, he was becoming more accustomed to the touch of others; the easy affection and open emotions of these people was infectious. "Hey, Jojo, Bohrm, it's Bel. Bel is who we were waiting on!"

Bohrm, whose scales had shifted to deep brown, nodded, stepping forward. He stayed silent, and Bel wondered if the man now believed Bel was who he said he was.

"Just you?" Bohrm said after a prolonged silence. "We were told that we would be getting the reinforcements we needed to take the island."

That would be a no then.

"We did," JoJo muttered joining the three of them. He looked for all the world like a small body builder, powerfully built but stubby. "Between the four of us, we shouldn't have any issue. We have the intelligence, the speed, and now we have the muscle. Combine all of that with the help we have been cultivating from the populace, we can do this."

Bohrm looked doubtful but nodded before looking Bel up and down as though trying to judge his strength and abilities simply through his physical body. "I assume you just got a general briefing on the islands, *Bel*?"

The reptilian Sheyd's tone grated against Bel. It was clear that not only did he not believe Bel was the figure he apparently idolized but he resented Bel for pretending to be. Such a bizarre form of hero worship as to despise the hero himself. Bel considered killing the Sheyd where he stood, but he doubted that such an act would help further his goals, or endear him to his other teammates.

"Yes, nothing specific to this island. I was told you would provide the weaponry necessary to do our jobs," Bel stated quietly—instead of gripping Bohrm's throat in his teeth and shaking him until his neck snapped.

Dara dropped his hand and walked towards a small table they had set up in the small campsite.

"For months, we've been scouting and infiltrating the people here. The good news is that they don't know that their *president* is a Watcher. They think he is a wizard."

"When I walked the Earth last, humans had dismissed magic, they called it the age of reason, the enlightenment. From what I was told in the City, that still holds true."

"It does, for the most part," Jojo offered. "See, places that separated from Earth proper, like the places within the mists, are different. Much of the magic that Earth lost is in these places, so the populace knows it exists. Some even use it, though it's rare to find humans doing so."

"There are also tribes and people who have not forgotten magic on Earth proper, it has just become very difficult for them to use." Bohrm grunted. "Wizards from Earth that get pulled into the mists tend to go mad with power pretty quickly. But we also have angels, Sheyd, and Malikim who seek the … freedom of the islands—renegades, rebels, criminals. My point is that there is no shortage of magic and danger here. I hope you are up for it."

Bel inwardly bristled at the implication but outwardly showed no signs of his annoyance. He just stared passively at the reptilian Sheyd.

Dara looked between the two of them. "Do you two want to just whip out your dicks and measure now or kiss or something? Because we do have a mission."

Jojo snickered and shook his head. "Look, you don't have to like Bohrm, and Bohrm, you don't have to believe or think anything about Bel you don't want to. But I am … I was the most veteran operative here, so maybe just trust me when I say we can trust Bel to pull his own weight."

"I trust you, Jojo, I just hope that General Agrat knows what the hell she is doing." He spat before walking away.

Bel almost stepped forward to follow the man and teach him a lesson in disrespecting his commanders, but Jojo shook his head.

"Give him time, Bel. He wants to win this war, it's important to him. He's just nervous that we can't. He lost his family to Watcher Jokabiel a couple of years ago, he's been obsessed with killing angels since, and he's good at it. But he hasn't had the opportunity to take down an actual Watcher yet."

"We have all lost loved ones in this war, satyr, all of us. It would be good for him to remember that we are allies and that putting one another down and sowing doubt is a gift the Watchers gave humanity."

Dara and Jojo didn't have a response to that; they stood in awkward silence for a moment. Dara almost looked like she wanted to say something when Bohrm came out of the underbrush at a mad dash.

"Ants!" he screamed

"Ants?" Bel asked, but Dara and Jojo were already grabbing armfuls of supplies and following Bohrm into the jungle. Underneath Bel's feet, the ground was shaking.

II

Bel was still watching the three Sheydim flee into the jungle when the first of the ants emerged from the underbrush. They were massive things. Great chitinous monsters that shouldn't be capable of existing under their own weight. But they were here. Bel roared his challenge as the first few emerged, his wings ripping from his back and stretching out, making him appear larger. It was a base instinct he was unable to quash entirely. The ants were easily the size of horses, and they were numerous.

Bel didn't hesitate; he leapt forward to meet the insects, smoke already billowing from his nostrils as he swung a claw at the first one he met. Within moments, they were swarming over him, the clacking mandibles snapping inches from his flesh as he moved between them. There were Sheydim who moved like smoke and water, flowing in battle as to never suffer the blade of an enemy. Bel was not those Sheydim. He was the unstoppable, the immovable, and he waded into the ants ringing out great blows that split chitinous heads apart with every blow. He ducked a massive warrior's head and came up under it, lifted the monstrous thing, and twisted, ripping the creature in half, then throwing it at its kin.

The stench of the things was overpowering. There were hundreds of them, and as fast as he whirled and struck out, there were always more. Bel inhaled, his chest expanding, before he belched a gout of flame. The insects screamed, or at least the steam of their vaporizing organs and blood escaping from between the plates of their exoskeleton sounded like screams. Bel reveled in the sound. The alien creatures cooked as easily as any other foe, and Bel's flames were as unending as his rage. He took another breath but was stopped short as a massive pair of mandibles snapped shut on his throat. A lesser being's head would have been severed. Bel reached up, grabbing the mandibles, trying to force them apart as he dangled off the ground.

"He's still here!" He heard the voice as if from a distance, barely a whisper over the sounds of the stampeding insects.

"Prince damn you, Bel!" another annoying voice.

But then a sound he had grown to recognize over the last few months. Gun shots. Rapid gun shots. The ant that had grabbed him dropped him and turned to face this new threat, only to come face to face with Bohrm's shotgun, which unloaded directly against its head, blowing chunks everywhere.

"About time you joined the battle," Bel growled, rubbing his throat.

"Yes, well, I don't know *why* we joined the damn battle!" he shouted back as he turned to fire another shot.

Bel noticed both Dara and Jojo were in the thick of it too. Dara carried a long, curved sword and was shooting ants with a large revolver similar to the ones he had seen before he died. Jojo carried some sort of massive barreled gun but was using it as a club and head-butting insects instead of firing.

"We need to go!" Dara called. "Habbiel will have sensed us by now!"

"We didn't need to fight the fucking ants!" Bohrm yelled again, still whining.

"We didn't need to, but we did. Your complaints are noted!" Jojo growled before charging past them once again, fleeing into the dense jungle.

"Bel! Come on!" Dara said, pausing next to him. "These are animals, not our enemies. We can't just fight everything, please."

He looked away from the encroaching ants to look at her. She was panting, her deep breaths causing her chest to strain at her clothes. The adrenaline of war getting his blood flowing, it was distracting. The best way to celebrate one conquest, was with another …

She cleared her throat, pulling his attention back to her face. "We need to go now!"

Snorting two small jets of flame, he turned away from the ants and followed Bohrm and Jojo into the jungle.

The four of them came to a breathless stop just by the side of the massive river after several long minutes of mad dash through the foliage. Jojo immediately moved to the river bank and began uncovering a small raft.

"We need to cross the river. The ants won't follow us past that once they lose our scent."

"Why do you fear the ants so? They are ants," Bel rumbled as he stood in stoic defiance of the nervousness the other Sheydim exuded.

"Holy shit, do you ever quit the tough guy act? Even for a damn second?" Bohrm growled as he pushed past Bel to help Jojo.

Bel took a step forward. He was exhausted of this petulant, disrespectful creature, and his blood still burned in the song of violence, a blood lust he had always had. Bel had inertia; once in motion, once moved to violence, he found it difficult to move past the siren call of bloodshed.

"No, Bel's right, because they are just ants and we could certainly have fought them all off," Jojo said, wiping sweat from his head. "Dara, can you finish getting the boat ready? I'll explain what's happening to Bel."

Dara nodded and took his place as the short satyr sighed and wiped his hands on his pants.

"I know it's been a while since you fought in the War. Look, if you really are who you claim to be …" he trailed off, trying to find the right words. "I know that it rankles you to not be leading the charge, I know it probably doesn't sit right to take orders. Technically, you outrank all of us, not in the hierarchy of the City's military, but in your strength and experience. I get all of that. But for this mission, specifically this mission, I'm leading. And I want you to trust me, I ask that you trust me, because I've been here longer, I know what's happening, and it would take a long time to explain everything to you, time we don't have." He watched Dara and Bohrm working and then turned back to Bel, who remained silent. "We do things for a reason. None of us are cowards, none of us are traitors, so if you see us retreating from a fight, no matter how alien that feels to you, just … trust we have a good reason."

"And the reason for this retreat?" Bel finally rumbled. His eyes were narrowed, a dim orange glow seeping through the lids. "Why flee ants?"

"The lesser Watchers love insects, they adore

swarms and controlling them. Those ants act as spies and scouts for Habbiel's military."

"Then we should destroy them!"

"No, he doesn't just see everything they see, but if something unusual happens, like a being in the middle of an uncivilized part of the jungle tears a bunch of them up barehanded and breathes fire, Habbiel *will* investigate that. Our job is to weaken Habbiel's hold on the people until he is weak enough for us to confront, for you to confront, and to do that, we need the elements of secrecy, surprise, and diplomacy."

Bel watched the satyr for a moment and then nodded. What he said made sense and mirrored what he had been told by Agrat and Lillith. He didn't understand stealth and covert operations. Not that they were new to the world, but as a dragon, he had never had cause to use those methods. Jojo looked relieved when Bel agreed.

"Come on, let's cross the river, we can finally formally introduce ourselves."

The four of them clambered onto the raft and set off across the massive river. It was crowded on the little dinghy; it had been intended for three, or even four, who were not Bel's size. Dara was pressed into Bel's chest, her petite backside soft against him. He still didn't trust the succubus, not entirely. They fed off lust and desire. He was nothing more than a means to an end for her. But it was pleasant. On the other side of Dara, Jojo used a long staff to steer them through the clear waters. And finally, Bohrm was at the other end, trying to keep all the gear they had managed to salvage before running from tumbling off the raft into the river.

"Okay …" Jojo sighed and pushed off the bottom of the river and looked around at his three companions. "So, you know us, or at least you know Dara, but what I think you need to understand, Bel, is that the islands, inside the mists, it's not like the rest of the human world."

Bel turned his orange eyes to the small satyr but remained silent. Dara wiggled against him, though whether trying to get comfortable or to flirt, he didn't know.

"Here, magic and mega fauna and violence are pretty standard, technology and magic merge, and really, if you think about it, it's more similar to back in East-of-Nod than anywhere else, except …"

"Except for the Watchers," Bohrm finished.

"Except for the Watchers," Jojo agreed. "They control everything. They are the gods here in a very real sense of the word, powered by the oppression they rain down on the sentient beings that live here."

"If they are so powerful here, then why would we come here to fight them?" Bel asked, irritated and distracted.

"Well, their power fluctuates more here," Dara said, looking up and twisting to meet his gaze. She placed a hand on his chest. "On Earth, when a Watcher grows to power, they can tap into the news, into social media, and tap into the adoration or fear of people worldwide. It makes them more … embedded. Here, if we topple the power structure under them, they are on their own. And then, a big, strong, badass Sheydim can stand toe-to-toe with the weakened angel."

"If their power is less sure … I do not understand the purpose of the islands then. Why would they want to cut themselves off?"

"The Watchers are egotistical sacks of shit," Bohrm finally spoke up. "If they are on Earth, they share in power with the other Watchers, that, and they can be spotted by Heaven. The last thing the fallen want is to have to face down Kamdiel or any of their own kin. Here, they have free reign, cut off from Heaven and their brothers, to just be whatever sort of asshole they want to be. It's just a lucky coincidence that it also cuts them off from the support they need to stay omnipotent."

"And how do we topple their power structure

then?" Bel asked.

Dara grinned up at him, her eyes glowing with an inner light as she answered, "Chaos."

III

"Dara here is our … expert in chaos," Jojo said with a sigh. "Sometimes I think it's something she enjoys too much, but …"

"But you are a demon, and she is Lillikim. She is formed of the stuff of creation melded with the chaos of humanity and the first woman," Bel finished for him. "You lead them, tell them which targets to hit and when?"

Jojo kept his head high and his eyes straight on the far riverbank as he steered the raft they rode. "Something like that, more like herding cats. But up until now, I was also the muscle, drawing fire and enemy attention so they could do what needed to be done. I'm happy to say that is now your job."

Bel didn't respond to that. It was not the first time he had been used as a distraction, it's what had gotten him killed centuries ago during the American Civil War. Instead, he jerked his chin towards Bohrm, his least favorite member of their little posse. "And him? If you are order and Dara is chaos, what is the Yokai?"

The reptilian Sheyd looked over his shoulder, a sour look on his face. He was surprised he had been identified from the one time Bel had seen him without a human disguise on. "Support," he said with a snort of dismissal.

Jojo nodded his agreement.

"Yep, Bohrm is support, long range support, to be specific. So, generally how it works is Dara and I make friends with the locals, figure out where potential allies are, where potential targets are, while Bohrm hangs back and covers us. Then we make friends, kill enemies, rinse, repeat until the island is ours in all but name. And then we lead someone who is a bit bigger and badder than us, like the prince, to the gates of the Watcher to take them down for good."

"Lucky for you, Mr. Bel …" Dara said, reaching up to adjust his collar—her body pressed into him by necessity of the small raft, but he was certain she was enjoying his discomfort. "We're done with the boring diplomacy bits already; we're ready to get straight onto the violence."

"That is lucky," he agreed.

"This time," Jojo interjected. "According to the General, we're not getting back up, meaning, Bel, you are our big guns. You are the bigger and badder thing we bring to the gates of the Grigori to trap them … I assume the prince provided you with a prison?"

"He did." Bel met Jojo's eyes, his blazing with an infernal orange light as if the fire in his belly roared throughout his skull. If any of these Sheyd thought he was going to bring the amulet Ashmandai had given him out before its appointed time, they were insane. Or at least seriously overestimating his trust in them.

The raft bumped into the far shore. Looking back the way they came, Bel could see the massive ants swarming on the far side of the river. Bel let a low growl rumble in his chest; he still wanted to kill the things. They were unnatural, they were servants of the enemy, he could smell the touch of the Grigori on them even from back here. It didn't surprise Bel that he would be taking on a role normally played by Ashmandai or Lillith. Though every Sheydim soul had been born in the twilight hours of the sixth day, they had been born into reality at different times. Ashmandai was the oldest of their kind, but Bel was not much younger. There were a few of them, or at least there had been. Bel wondered about the other ancients. Did Tanin'iver yet live? The mother of vengeance and blades had been captured and locked in a magical prison by Azazel, last he had known. He assumed Mammon yet lived, but he was a traitor, a creature of greed and pain that had gone willingly to serve with the Grigori. Perhaps he would get to break the traitor's neck himself. Bel smiled as he considered the possibilities of destroying those Sheydim that had embraced the darkness of the enemy.

The four of them unloaded from the raft,

grabbing what supplies they had saved from the marching insects. Bel watched the three he had been assigned to, wondering what Agrat had been thinking. He had yet to see them in action, and he knew better than to judge a spirit by its appearance. But in the old days, fighting against the Grigori had involved armies of Sheydim. They had marched in thousands against the creatures, alongside angels like Kamdiel and Domah, with the full might of Lillith and Ashmandai at the fore, and still they had lost battles.

Now four—a satyr, a kappa, and a succubus, and himself, the very last Dragon—would take on the might of one of the first shards of divinity to ever exist, and to ever be corrupted. It would appear to be a lost cause. But he doubted that the six-fingered prince would send him to his death so swiftly after he had spent his forces so dearly to save him. Bel sighed to himself and finally moved to carry some of the heavier equipment.

"Where do we go now?" he asked Jojo as he hefted a large flat box onto his shoulder and followed after the strange trio.

"There is a military fort up ahead. We were going to skip it and maybe do some smaller camps first, work our way up, but since the ants disrupted our location, we might as well go big," Jojo answered.

"I prefer it this way." Dara giggled. "I hate going after those small camps."

"It's necessary, Dara. Every strike against Habbiel is worth the time." Jojo grunted as if explaining things to a child.

"I didn't say I didn't get it, I said it's boring," she said, mocking his matter-of-fact tone.

"Of course you think it's boring," Bohrm said. "Not chaotic enough, you hate me showing you up."

"I do not. You couldn't do wha—"

"What is our current target?" Bel interrupted their bickering.

Jojo sat at the base of the tree that Bohrm had climbed. He seemed completely calm, taking the moment to rest with his eyes closed as though conserving his energy. Bel stood, ramrod straight, in the center of a moonbeam that fell through the foliage overhead. He was agitated. When they had arrived, Jojo had halted them just inside the tree line separating the dense jungle from the military base in the clearing. They had sat there doing nothing for hours, just waiting for night to fall. Bel didn't have any issue with that, he understood the value of striking at night, but as soon as darkness fell, Bohrm had unpacked some sort of long, thin gun and climbed the tree he was now in. Dara had packed a bag of supplies, hidden her shocking hair under a black watch cap, and then headed towards the camp.

Bel had started to follow when Jojo put a hand on his shoulder and shook his head.

"Dara goes in first, softens things up. Trust us. We know what we are doing."

Bel had not responded but had taken up his spot and locked his eyes on Dara's retreating form. She was soon lost to the shadows, even to his superb night vision. He lifted his gaze to the tree where Bohrm and his gun sat. He couldn't see the Yokai either. "Can he see her?"

"Yeah, he has a scope that allows him to see heat signatures." Jojo cracked open an eye. "I'm surprised you can't do that. Don't snakes hunt using heat?"

"I'm not a snake."

"Well, I mean reptiles, reptiles do that."

"I'm not a reptile any more than you are a goat. Don't fall into the trap of assuming my biology is in any way designated by the laws and physics governing mortal creatures."

"Ah, I guess I just assumed that any gift available to a mortal would be something you had," Jojo stammered, though in truth, he had always assumed that classifications worked for Sheydim. After all, Jojo was a mammal, even if he was a magical creature. Why would the dragon *not* be a reptile?

Bel offered Jojo a small smile. "Flattering, but no, I can't hunt by heat signature. Snakes use that because they are stealthy, cunning hunters. I am not a creature of stealth, Jojo."

"No, I suppose not." He looked up into the tree. "Status?"

"Lots of guards," came Bohrm's voice from the dense foliage. "She's taking her time ... they keep almost coming up on her."

"I should go in there ..." Bel said, turning back towards the base.

"Bel ... wait."

But Bel didn't want to wait. He had not worked with these people, and he would not lose a team member the first time they encountered a true enemy. He could raze this base in the blink of an eyes, tearing it board from board with tooth and claw. He was just stepping out of the tree line when several explosions suddenly ripped through the base. There was screaming, and the smell of burning flesh and fuel filled the air. He took three steps forward and almost ran into Dara, who was trotting back towards them.

"Oh!" Dara exclaimed, surprised to run into him. She pressed her hands against his chest, smiling up, her white teeth almost glowing in the darkness of the night backlit by the burning base. "Don't worry, I've left some for you. But I destroyed their communications array. You ready to play?"

Bel looked up from the succubus and at the base, where he could hear someone shouting orders over the sound of crackling and burning.

"Absolutely," he answered.

IV.

The army camp blazed. Several humans were running and screaming, trying to find the source of the explosions. There had been unrest on the island, of course. There were always those who bucked against Habbiel's tyrannical rule, but they had never had the nerve to strike directly like this before. It was chaos. Not one soldier, from the base's lowliest guard to the commander who oversaw it all, had ever expected to be attacked inside the base. Many were already dead, caught by shrapnel, gas, and flames.

The guards and soldiers didn't realize that the explosions were only the prelude to true terror.

Bel charged. He hadn't grabbed any weapons, he didn't need to, his body was his weapon. From somewhere behind him, he heard Jojo curse. If the little goat man wanted to take his time and be careful, that was fine. But Bel had spent months trainings and going through practice drills. He wanted to taste destruction and violence without limits. He reached the panicked soldiers in seconds, a living shadow of claws and rage among the blood and fear of the humans. His talon-tipped hand flashed out, catching a man along the side, caving his chest and tearing out several ribs. Bel was already turning, burying his claws in the next soldier's mouth, reaching down his throat to grab his heart, the man's skin ripping as Bel forced his arm past the man's limits of elasticity.

Ripping his arm free, bisecting the man, Bel brought the heart to his lips and tore off a large bite. The man's life filled his head as he feasted on the fleshy meat of the organ. He knew the dead man, his sins, his few victories, his secrets …

Around him, the soldiers were screaming, trying to rally. A few even took shots at the killer in their midst, but with all the chaos, as many bullets hit their allies as came near Bel. And those few shots that did hit Bel had no chance of penetrating the body armor and his scaly hide. Bel's eyes were an infernal orange light as he waded into the melee, tossing men aside like broken things as he shoved his way through the crowd, eviscerating any who stood in his path.

Dara stood at the edge of town watching him, mouth agape. She had doubted that he would actually be able to stand toe-to-toe against one of the Grigori, but now, watching him tearing apart the soldiers as though they were made of wet paper rather than flesh and bone made her second guess that doubt. Jojo sauntered up beside her and brought his chaingun to bear. The barrels spun up to speed and began spitting enchanted lead into the dense crowd of humans, tearing them apart. Every few moments, a loud pop would sound and a soldier's head would explode as Bohrm took another shot. Over the sound of screams, gunshots, and the constant crackling of the flames, Bel's laughter carried across the battlefield.

Suddenly, a bright light appeared over the trees, crashing down to Earth like a comet, cracking the earth and sending humans flying in all directions. **"ENOUGH! BE NOT FOOLS. FEAR ME."** The voice boomed from the figure, a titanic humanoid whose flesh crackled with black flames. All over its body, flesh opened, revealing a blinking eye before the eye closed and the flesh sealed over again. This was an angel, not one of the Grigori, but a lesser creature. One of the plague of heavenly servants who fell in service to the lustful degenerates. Human flesh melted near the creature, running like rivulets down their faces as eyes burst and hair caught on fire in proximity to the black conflagration.

Dara yelped as she fell back away from the angel, and even Jojo spat a curse as he let his gun spin down. An angel was another matter. Even those lesser creatures were terribly strong. They possessed a brutal strength and magic ability far superior to anything the humans could muster. Bohrm cursed as well, trying to figure out the best way to delay the angel so his friends, and Bel, could escape the monster.

Bel was unimpressed. He certainly wasn't afraid of the melodramatic show the angel was mounting; it was murdering its own loyal servants in an attempt to garner the upper hand. Bel stalked forward, his body growing more draconic with each step, and punched the angel in the face. The black flames licked harmlessly at his Sheyd flesh as the divine messenger stumbled back from the blow.

Dara and Jojo paused in their flight, watching, mouths agape, as Bel struck the divine creature.

"You dare?" he spat, lifting a hand to his already swelling cheek. **"You would strike an angel of the lord, a servant of your god Habbiel?"**

Bel spat out a laugh. "I do not bow to the Creator of the universe, I will not bow to a splintered shard of a pitiful, petulant child." He grabbed the angel's shoulder, his thumb digging into one of the eyes as it opened there. The angel screamed. Bel used the grip to lift the angel from the ground and throw him into the side of a burning building.

The angel emerged from the flame, golden glittering blood leaking slowly from his shoulder. He limped a little; the force of the throw had harmed him. He was unused to things hurting him. **"You are Sheyd ..."** He said it almost as an accusation.

"Habbiel warned me of your half-born breed, he warned me about you, you and your prince. Do you really think a mere Sheyd can harm me?"

"It must be difficult maintaining that lie when you are already bleeding and whining like a struck puppy. Normally, now I would tell you to limp back to your master, give him tidings, but no … I think instead I am hungry."

"Your threats are empty, you cannot hurt me, and you most certainly cannot eat m—"

His words broke off into a scream as Bel leapt forward and dragged the angel to the ground with his teeth, which were growing longer and sharper by the second. Bel did not relent, ripping and tearing great chunks of meat out of him and swallowing them raw. The thick golden blood oozed down his throat as he devoured the flesh greedily.

The surviving humans ran screaming from the scene as the reptilian Sheyd devoured the angel alive, the once-divine thing screaming in agony, rage, and terror until there was no longer enough left of it to scream. Bel stood, coated in the golden angelic blood. The demons and Dara stood several feet away staring at him in equal measures of awe and horror. Even Bohrm had come down from his tree and stood with the others. Bel looked down at himself, disgusted by the blood on him. He glanced up for the first time since his fight began and took in the looks he was getting from his team members.

"What?" he growled as his teeth shrank and his body twisted and cracked into its more human semblance. When he was finished, he looked around. The ground was coated in corpses and blood, fires still raged, but the soldiers had long since fled.

"What … the … fuck?" Bohrm finally managed to mutter.

Bel ignored him and began marching back towards the river. "I'm going to go get cleaned up," he said, ignoring the looks he was getting.

Bel sighed in the cool waters of the river. It was soothing against his skin. The angelic blood burned, it sizzled against his flesh. It sat heavy in his stomach too, but he could deal with that. He was designed to devour. He was Jörmungandr, he was the Tarrasque, the devourer.

"Bel?"

Bel turned in the water, unbothered by his nudity, his human shape fully on display. Dara raised an eyebrow at the display but then looked back to his face. "What?" he asked.

"I wanted to check on you, make sure you were okay." She reached up and began pulling her own body armor and clothes off, tossing them on the river's sandy banks next to his.

"What are you doing?" he asked, though he didn't look away. She was an extremely attractive woman. Where Lillith was strength and softness, Dara was entirely hard, a well-muscled gymnast who would be as much a warrior as she was anything else.

"I'm joining you," she answered, peeling her panties off before reaching back and freeing herself from the confines of her bra.

"I am fine."

"Yeah, you are." She grinned, stepping into the water, her pouty lips turning into an *O* in surprise at the cold. "You shocked us, is all, fighting an angel on, well, more than even footing. It's a lot, and then ... the brutality."

"You find it objectionable?" he asked as she swam towards him.

She reached him and put her hands on his waist, steadying herself before pressing in closer, purring as her hand slid down his body and stroked him. "Do I seem like I find it objectionable?"

Bel tilted his head. He could stop this, step back, push her away, but the truth was that it had been too long since he had enjoyed taking a lover. Dara was attractive, she was capable of chaos and war. And she offered herself her willingly. He finally shook his head.

"No, you do not seem to be put off." He placed his hands on her waist, his palms exploring her skin, playing across her taut stomach, and reaching around to give her pert ass a squeeze.

Bohrm rolled his eyes, listening to the moans and shouts coming from the river. "They're going to give our position away."

Jojo glanced at Bohrm and shrugged. "You tell him that. You know Dara, when she wants something, she goes for it. Sounds like he wanted it too. Besides, he just ate a fucking angel. Habbiel won't take that lying down. We need to figure out our next steps."

V.

Bel walked back towards the fort. Jojo and Bohrm were sifting through the wreckage, cataloging the dead and, maybe most importantly, trying to discern what sorts of weaponry the soldiers had wielded before Bel had ripped them apart. Behind him, a few feet away, Dara followed a little crookedly in his wake. Jojo nodded his greeting, but Bohrm couldn't hold his tongue.

"Satisfied with yourself?"

Bel paused and tilted his head, silently watching the Kappa, his orange eyes languid and dim in his post-coital haze.

"I don't know about with himself, but he satisfied me," Dara quipped, grinning as she passed Bel and blew Jojo a kiss.

Bel cracked a lazy smile. He was satisfied with himself. He had murdered an angel and then had enjoyed every inch of a succubus's body and skill all in an afternoon.

"Well, I hope you didn't wear yourselves out, we should move before Habbiel sends reinforcements or checks up on his messenger."

"Would that not be a perfectly reasonable method of drawing out the angel?" Bel asked.

"If you want to fucking die, then yeah, it's fine," Bohrm snarled. "Try to use your brain for something other than fighting and fucking, Sheyd. Just because we destroyed this fort doesn't mean we've lowered Habbiel's influence at all. We have to spread the word first; we have to get it out there that this happened. We have to destroy more forts, we have to convince the people of this island that they have the power to break Habbiel's control, and then we can march up to his palace and be killed by him in person."

Bel took a step forward, his post-orgasm high dissipating in the light of Bohrm's snide tone.

Jojo stepped between them.

"While he says it like an asshole, he's not wrong. What we did here was important, and you, both of you, more than earned your rest and fun. But we still have to play smart because we can't all go toe-to-toe like you can, and we can't free the people of this island by being reckless."

Bel snorted, a plume of smoke rising from his nostrils before he nodded. While he sorely wanted to put the Kappa in his place, he was no impulsive teenager who would endanger the mission that his prince and queen had entrusted to him. But even their trust in him mattered less than vengeance. He fought in this war not for others but for his people. The dragons who had died at the tips of angelic blades. He would not allow this strutting turtle-demon, nor his own loins, to muddy the waters of his intention. He nodded his acknowledgment of Jojo's words and moved past the two men to look over the place where he had murdered an angel.

There were feathers strewn about. Though some might think it monstrous, the truth was that weapons made of the remains of the heavenly host were often sought after, or least they had been before his "death." Bel knelt in the gore and began gathering the feathers up; they could be used to fletch arrows or woven into a cloak. The magic of creation saturated even these meager clumps of fallen detritus, and it should not go to waste.

If he had been less impulsive on the battlefield, they could have gathered the creature's teeth and bones. They could be ground up and mixed with gun powder, a trick he had learned in China centuries ago. Too late now. He glanced up at Dara as she gingerly stepped over a severed arm to pick up an ammo belt of grenades that had somehow managed not to explode. He admired her for a moment before frowning and turning away; he was far too old to become infatuated with a woman just because they had taken a roll together. He was also keenly aware that while his nature was one of slow plodding destruction and inevitability, Dara was a creature born of chaos, with all the passion of Lillith and all the capriciousness of Ashmandai. He looked down at the feathers in his hand before making his way back towards the other men.

"Where next then? My blood is hot, and I am hungry for death."

"Hungry?" Bohrm actually looked shocked. "You just ate! You just ate a fucking angel."

"The problem with divine beings, an hour later …" He grinned, unable to resist pouring salt into Bohrm's wounded pride. "Besides, I worked up an appetite."

Bohrm rolled his eyes, throwing his hands up in surrender. "Fine, fine, let's get going then. This was the closest, but now that the angels know we're here, we need to be pretty strategic." He squatted down in the dirt and used a clawed finger to draw a map in the earth.

Jojo nodded and plopped down on his ass, grabbing a stick to draw a few circles on the map. "They'll expect us to stay hidden in the jungle and hit these easy targets."

"Which they will reinforce, thus making them less … easy." Bohrm interjected.

"Right, but there isn't much of a point in taking these smaller hidden bases out anyway. We need to target something that will get the people's attention more than the angels'."

Bel looked at the map for a moment, studying their options, and then joined them in the dirt. "Here," he said, gesturing with a claw at one of the circles. "This one, I saw it during my descent. It is located next to a large settlement."

"Yeah, that would be one of the biggest military installments on the island. We were thinking once we had gathered enough support, we could take it out as a prelude to going after Habbiel," Jojo explained.

Bel shook his head. "No, it's next to the city, meaning it has buildings that Bohrm can use as vantage points. We can sow chaos in the base before Dara even begins her unique touch to things. If we destroy this, this symbol of the angel's might and superiority, we will inspire the people towards rebellion that much faster."

"But the risk is great, the angels and their allies will be all over this one. This one will have far more immortals, demons, Sheydim; you name it, you'll find it there."

"Bohrm can easily take out the largest threats before they know they are being hit. You told me yourself that he was good at killing angels," Bel countered. "Dara's explosive expertise will ensure they are unable to organize, and then you and I will wipe out the rest of the base easily. Imagine the mortals' feelings! They watch the four of us, just the four of us, take on the might of his armies without fear, they will have our backs, they will switch their awe from Habbiel to us, and then dissent and rebellion will spread like wildfire across the island."

Jojo opened his mouth and then closed it. Bohrm seemed mollified by Bel's trust in his abilities. They hadn't thought they could possibly take such an intimidating target without first raising an army, but after seeing the carnage Bel had unleashed, there was actual hope that they could do this, that they could, in fact, dismantle Habbiel's power structure that much faster.

Dara approached, grinning and lifting the large bazooka over her diminutive form. She looked almost comical, but from the wicked smile plastered on her face, the result of her find would be anything but comical. "Did I hear you guys right? Are we actually going to start this party for real?"

"That is what Bel is proposing," Bohrm answered, his eyes not budging from the ebony skinned dragon. "He thinks the four of us are up for the challenge. What do you think?" he asked, turning his head to meet Dara's eyes.

Bel had expected her to exuberantly back the play, but to his surprise, she set the weapon down and stared at the map thoughtfully. "I think that it would be extremely dangerous, possibly suicidal. But the General told me she once watched a lone gunman take on an Army base in America with nothing more than a revolver, a sword, and a couple of sticks of TNT." She shrugged.

"Yeah, what happened?" Bohrm asked.

"He was joined by an army of indigenous people and then got captured by an extremely powerful Sheyd. But my point is that that man was just a mortal, a human. We aren't, we are the extremely powerful Sheydim, or ... beings, in this scenario. Jojo? It's your call, but I believe that we can conquer this place."

Over the sounds of the jungle, a horn blew a single, mournful note as though from a massive shofar. The note floated above the trees and echoed across the coast.

"Habbiel is mobilizing his forces. He knows that one of his servants has been killed. We need to move before they start flooding in here. We'll find a safe spot, eat, and rest," Jojo decided before rising.

"Yeah, not all of us just ate an entire being," Bohrm said with a laugh, his first warm comment towards Bel.

"I dunno, I worked up an appetite," Dara said. "Blowing things, up or otherwise," she shot Bel a devious smile, "tends to make me hungry."

"I could eat again," Bel admitted.

Jojo rolled his eyes with a sigh. They were incorrigible. "Let's go."

The four of them—demons, Lillikim, and Sheyd—all rose and gathered their things, moving quickly into the underbrush. Bel fell into a morose mind set again. He shouldn't get attached to these three; they were frail in comparison to him, and their task was great. It was likely that one or all of them might die in the coming battle, and if they did survive … Would they be able to survive the savagery of a Watcher? Dragons, by their very nature, were solitary creatures, but that did not stop them from amassing a following, a harem of lovers and servants who doted on the mighty creatures. A few of his kind had even taken mates, consorts. It always ended badly; the eternal devourers were not meant for camaraderie.

He glanced at Jojo and Bohrm. They would make fine warriors, and now that he had seen them in battle and understood their roles, he could understand why Agrat had sent them here. Dara was likewise resourceful and dangerous, but he was loathe to lift her on a pedestal. He was all too familiar with how intimacy could make one blind to faults and lead to tragedy. A succubus, more than any other, would pull at desire and longing to create that connection. It would not even be conscious; she may want nothing more than a quick fuck in the river, but her nature would create chemical and magical reactions to strengthen his desire and infatuation with her. He had to guard against it. He had been stabbed in the back by lovers past, and while he doubted Dara had any such malicious designs on him, he did not wish to let her hold on him create a weakness that could be exploited. Nor did he wish to experience pain or heartbreak when she eventually fell in battle.

He resolved to distance himself from the grip of the succubus, perhaps separate himself from this group after they had overthrown Habbiel. With this in mind, he straightened his back and pushed through the trees to find a good spot to camp for the night.

VI.

The four creatures walked through the streets of the Illaatian city. Through glamour and cloaks, they hid their nature from the mortal humans surrounding them. They came to a stop across the street from the military installation and watched the activity inside for a moment. The soldiers and guards were mobilizing, gathering together to ride into the jungle and hunt down the dangerous rebels who had begun sowing dissent and chaos. Of course, they wouldn't find anything in the jungle. Their quarry was already hunting them.

Bel's orange eyes moved over the razor wire fence of the base, taking in the meager defenses. They were laughable. These were the defenses of a group that knew they had nothing to fear from mortals. Despite the deterrents set in place for mere humans, Bel understood that this would not be as simple as the last fort. Here there would be more dangerous prey. More able combatants. Even considering that the majority of the base seemed to be emptying out, there would still be real muscle inside. At least, Bel was assuming there would be. Hoping. There would be little point in taking out this base if everyone of import was gone. A delicate balancing act of risk and reward. But delicate was not his forte.

"Bohrm, that building, I feel it would give the best angle," Bel finally said. He didn't know much about sniper rifles, or the act of long-distance terrorism, but he did know about scouting from great heights.

Bohrm looked over the building for a moment, a gaudy thing of gold and steel that rose like an unnatural growth above the island. "Probably too tall from the roof, but if I took an angle from one of the mid-level windows … yeah." He slipped away, leaving the three of them alone, waiting for the first shots to ring out.

After a few moments, Dara pressed against Bel's side, leaning her head on him. He stiffened but didn't push her away. "Bohrm can be an asshole—I know I keep saying that—but he's not a bad person. He's good at his job, and he wants what's best for East-of-Nod." She looked up at him, her eyes shimmering and prismatic, born of equal parts shadow and life.

He watched her eyes for a moment, comparing them in his head to the precious jewels in his horde that had been lost to his centuries-long slumber. He frowned ever so slightly and looked away from her, raising his eyes to the towering buildings around them.

"I trust he will use his judgment on when to

begin his assault," Bel answered, resisting the urge to reach around the diminutive woman and pull her closer. "Then you will take the next steps."

"While they're all panicking and trying to find the sniper, I'll use the opportunity to lay down some explosive charges where they can do the most damage, and use the laser to paint targets for Bohrm. But … it's going to be more dangerous than before, Bel, a lot more dangerous. I'll need cover."

"Don't worry about that," Jojo jutted in. "I'll be going in with you to cover your back. We want to hold off on Bel making an appearance until the last moment. We want them to be overconfident right up until they lose all hope; it will have a greater effect on the humans that way too." He turned to Bel. "Does that make sense to you? Waiting until their sure they've won and then—"

"And then crushing that arrogance," Bel finished. "It does, but I will not hesitate to join the fray if it looks like you will fall," he added. "No losses, no deaths, not here. I have no desire to return to the City and inform my prince that my team fell in battle."

Jojo smirked a little. "Well, I suppose that's what passes for camaraderie from wyrms." He glanced at Dara, who was watching Bel thoughtfully. "Come on, Dara, let's start finding a place where we can move quickly once Bohrm starts shooting.

Bel, I won't tell you where to make your ingress, I just ask that you make it showy, give the humans something to rally behind. And maybe don't devour any angels. It might scare people too badly."

Bel blinked slowly at the small stocky satyr but nodded. He had a point. Bel was a devourer, an eater of civilizations. But he was also a tactician, a creature who craved victory more than the fleeting satiation of a hunger that could never truly be filled. He stepped back and turned away from the garrison. He would find somewhere he could watch the unfolding chaos in comfort. This would be a true battle. Though all of them were discussing this as something that could be done, the truth was that now the Watcher's servants would be alert, angels especially could return to join the battle swiftly.

Angels presented another problem for their mission. Angels inspired awe in humans, a near animal panic and reverence through their mere existence. For this reason, Bel would need to make an entrance that arrested attention. He would need to be a spectacle, wrench the people's worshipful eyes off of the false saviors and fill their hearts with awe. He noticed a small cart on the street corner, surrounded by rickety tables and chairs. A street vendor. Bel smiled and ordered food, surprised to find it was simply roasted corn on a stick smothered in some kind of white sauce, juice from a citrus, and spices. He had hoped for a hot dog. Bel sat in one of the chairs and watched the skies for his prey.

Bel was halfway through his elotes, enamored with the taste and texture of the meal, when he heard the first gunshot, followed by the first scream. Languidly, he raised his eyes to the base to see the soldiers running around in a panic. He was a bit frustrated; he had finally found some food worth eating on this trip, other than Dara, and now his meal was being interrupted by work. But such was life. He scanned the skies, but of course it was too soon for any reinforcements to show up, and so he turned his gaze to the base itself, orange eyes searching for any sign of Dara and Jojo making their move.

The whole time, shots rang out. Each shot resulted in more screams, more shouts. Finally, the soldiers began firing back. Judging from tracer fire, none of them seemed to have a clear idea where the sniper was.

From his vantage point in front of the base, Bel couldn't see if Dara was painting targets for Bohrm to take out, but the regularity of the shots made him think that perhaps they weren't doing a very good job of seeking cover. As an explosion ripped through the back of the base, Bel brought the corn back to his mouth and tore the sweet kernels off, reveling in the mix of sweet corn, tangy lime, subtle heat from the chilies, and umami of the sauce. He wondered if he could get elotes in the City East-of-Nod. They seemed to have everything else, a different vendor selling a different ethnic food on every corner, exotic things like hot dogs and tacos. Corn on a stick would fit right in.

Bel watched the flames licking the sky and the thick black plumes of smoke rising from the base. All around him, humans were gathering to stare at the chaos happening just a few meters away. Human instinct to watch chaos unfolding. But Bel paid them little mind, his attention was on the other shapes racing across the sky, the angels. They were coming. Bel sighed, looking around. Seeing a small human child, he knelt before them, offering the food. "Here, child, I cannot finish this."

The young girl stared up at him for a moment, taken aback by his jet black skin and the slightly glowing orange eyes that revealed themselves in the shadows of his cowl. Slowly, she took the food and smiled, too shy to vocalize her thanks. Bel had always liked children more than adults. They understood what was important.

Bel pushed his way out of the gathering throng to approach the army base. He was about to throw off his disguise and take to the air when he saw one of the approaching flying figure's head explode and the thing drop like a stone to the ground. It was close enough that he could hear the sickening smack of wet meat slapping the earth and the shattering of bones. Music to his ears. But the other angels had also noticed, and they changed trajectory. They knew where Bohrm was.

Bel crouched and then sprang into the air. The cloak he wore transformed into great leathery wings as he lifted, and he wanted to fully transform, to crush the base under talon and tail, to roar to the heavens and shake this false paradise. But he was a weapon best held in reserve. It was best to not let Habbiel know what was coming until it was too late. With a flap of his wings, Bel soared towards the skies. The angels were so focused on their target, they didn't notice the black shape approaching until he was among them. The humans could only watch as the predatory Bel tore into the fallen host of heaven high above them. The first angel he came across was almost human looking, except for the wings of pure light and the skin covered in fingernails. Bel crashed into him full force and, with a rake of his claws, tore bloody furrows in the keratin armor.

The angel screamed its fury, turning to lash at Bel with a sword crafted from sordid words. The other angels turned to face this new threat, but Bel was on top of the angel too quickly. He planted his feet on the angel's chest and gripped his head between his claws, then, kicking and wrenching, ripped the angel's head free. The body, headless and gushing golden blood in a grisly spiral as it tumbled, fell to earth to join its fellow. The other angels hovered in the air, shock and disbelief warring on their inhuman faces. Bel looked at the head in his hands and causally let it roll off his fingers and plummet downward, then turned his eyes towards the other angels.

"Shall we begin?" he asked, flames licking between his teeth.

VII.

Above Habbiel's burning army base, Bel, the last dragon, lazily flapped his wings, hovering in the air, surrounded on all sides by the lesser angels that served the Watcher. Beneath them, flames raged from several explosions that Bel's team had unleashed upon the more terrestrial bound soldiers. From a nearby office building, the occasional shot rang out, fired by Bohrm. But no angel dared turn their back on the Sheyd that flew in front of them. They had, each of them, felt the messy, grisly death of their brother shredded by his teeth. They had heard about all that was left behind. Bel had eaten the angel alive.

They feared him even before he had flown into their midst and ripped the head off one of their kind and thrown it down to the streets below them. But Bel was outnumbered. There were five angels, each armed with divine weapons, swords and axes crafted by Habbiel himself, who in turn had learned the art of weapon craft from Azazel the Warmonger. And Bel was unarmed. For the most part. He had claws and he had teeth. Though he appeared like a winged human, his slit orange eyes gave truth to the fact he was an insidiously dangerous Sheyd.

They attacked as one. Angels could communicate through thought, acting as one being. They, more than the Sheydim, were legion, a gestalt hive mind of disgusting winged vultures picking at the decaying flesh of the Creator's worlds. They came at him from all angles. In the air, there were 360 degrees of attacks, and Bel knew them all. He was the wyrm in the deepest sea and the leather raptor of the clouds. He whirled in the windstorm of rushing wings, lashing out with talon-tipped fingers to tear into the iron-hard flesh of the Ish'im. He laughed as he moved through their clumsy attempts at attack. They were used to fighting humans and lesser beings. Centuries of complacency made them slow.

"Come now, Messengers, Watcher's worthless winged whelps! Bring the impotent fury of your importance to me. Fall to my teeth, my claws. Your mastery is at an end!"

Immediately in the chaos of the angels' rush, one was eviscerated, his golden entrails sloshing out to tumble downward. The disemboweled angel dropped his sword and went limp, consciousness failing and the forces of gravity finishing Bel's grisly work. Before the sword could tumble, Bel reached out and grabbed the blade, swinging it through the air to counter another angel's attack. Bel flapped his wings, trying to get above the cloud of shining feathers and strike down, but the angels came with him.

Bel parried another slash, forcing the blade up, and with a twist of his wings, he maneuvered behind the offending angel and bit deep into her neck where it joined at the shoulder. His teeth, sharp and serrated, tore into the holy flesh easily. He ripped his head back and tore out most of her throat. The angel, inhumanely beautiful, who had lured many humans into infidelity and degenerate acts of debasement, wailed as her gushing golden blood geysered out, leaving her too weak to maintain altitude. She joined the messy splotches of divinity littering the streets beneath the melee. Wiping the blood off his face with his sleeve, Bel dodged two more attacks.

Despite himself, he knew he may have bitten off more than he could chew. Angels, for all their weaknesses, had infinite stamina. They could fly and combat Bel until the end of the worlds if they needed to. Bel was already growing tired, the aerial combat draining his reserves of energy. But he would be damned and dead if he showed weakness to these lesser beings. These pretenders to decadence, these were merely the remora that followed in the wake of the Grigori. Despicable and terrible in their own, but less than specs of dust in the grand scheme of the War of Dictates.

Bel blocked and deflected the blades of the three angels as they surrounded him. Each swing sapped his strength but revealed more of their patterns. Bel was not simply a beast of war; he had survived since the birth of creation through his strength, yes, but also through his wits. He was a tactician as well as a devourer. He slid through their defenses, scoring tiny knicks here and there. Trading a small scratch for a vicious blow. Blood, both angelic gold and draconic black, fell to the earth as the four beings as old as time raged.

Bel had fought besides angels as well as against them, and he remembered a lesson taught by Kamdiel, one of the Creator's angriest and most loyal angels. Seeing his opportunity, Bel feinted and then dropped, folding his wings and plummeting several feet before catching himself. The angels, single-minded and focused entirely on striking the dragon dead, had lunged at the perceived opening. Two angels skewered one another and stared in shock and horror as their bloods mingled. They were siblings, lovers, comrades, and now they were each other's murderers as well. Bel's smirk widened into a toothsome grin as the two angels joined their dead kind on the ground. Now, numerically, things were even, and no minor angel was the match of Bel.

"Do not presume to have won, little Sheyd!"

the final divine insect bellowed, swinging its singing khopesh in a downward strike that dug into Bel's shoulder. Bel winced as black blood boiled from his wound. **"There is no safety for you here. There is no place that you and your kind can hide from the Watchers. We see all, we are all!"**

Bel ground his lengthening teeth together. "Little?" he growled, swelling, inhuman muscles pushing through the thin fabric of false flesh. "Who is little, you fucking pigeon?"

The fighting below slowed as Bel's shadow grew, swallowing the army base below. Every passing moment revealed the reptilian form of the mighty dragon. The beast was sinuous, massive enough to swallow a horse whole. His wings cast shadows as long as buildings. With a mighty flap of those wings, he sent the lesser angel spinning away through the air. One massive claw reached out and grabbed the angel as it tumbled.

"Am I so little?" Bel lifted the angel above his head, opened his maw impossibly wide, and let loose a gout of flame as long as a river, roasting the angel in his hand.

The screams lasted seconds before his angelic vocal cords were too charred to work any longer. Bel released the now wingless angel, still living, still burning, to tumble to the ground and shatter like spent charcoal against the asphalt below.

"You were never a Watcher," Bel murmured as he watched the grisly scene. "And your masters are nothing."

All of the angels who had come flocking to the chaos in the base were dead. Bel finally turned his attention below, to his comrades. Dara, easily visible because of her brightly colored hair, was laughing gleefully as she mowed down another group of soldiers with an automatic rifle. Jojo was weaving in and out of close combat against a spindly demon. It had too many arms, looking like someone had tried to shove a man-sized spider into the blood-drained pallid corpse of a long-limbed man. He recognized that demon. Bel glanced up towards the building where Bohrm had made his nest, unbothered and safe in his little hidey-hole. Bel shrank, allowing his true form to collapse in on itself, allowing his onyx scales to smooth into the dark skin once more before he folded his wings in and dove to join the others below.

Landing with a crash, he took a moment to take in the carnage. Despite their claims of the danger this place posed, they had unleashed a special kind of hell on the unsuspecting base. Dara looked like she had yet to be touched by any blade, bullet, or hand. And while Jojo sported a black eye and several rips in his clothes from talon and knife, he was still grinning and hadn't slowed yet. The corpses of many men and demons lay near him. Those that had gotten close enough to harm him had paid with their lives.

Bel assessed the situation and charged forward into the melee. The thing fighting Jojo looked even more spider-like close-up. His face was a pallid mask of skin stretched over mandibles. Unnatural eyes with starburst pupils jutted from stretched holes all over the man's head. Bel smiled grimly, reaching forward to grab the demon, but with eyes in the back of its head, it wasn't so easy, and the thing dodged out of the way.

Jojo nodded his greeting but said nothing as he adjusted his grip on his knives. The two men traded swipes with the demon, an intricate dance of blade and talon, with neither side gaining the upper hand. Despite battling the angels in the air, this demon was older, faster, and more experienced in fighting. The three of them were cautious. Despite having survived his wounds, Jojo knew he didn't have the strength to finish the fight if he took any more hits, and Bel knew from experience how deadly this particular entity could be. He was fast and unhurt too, and Bel wondered if it was toying with them.

To do so would be a grave mistake. Bel's lips twisted into a grim scowl. Mocking a dragon never went well. He was about to roar his challenge and initiate the change to a more natural shape when suddenly the demon collapsed in a spray of blood and bone as his legs were shredded by distant rifle fire. Bel glanced up to where Bohrm was hidden, it was a perfect shot.

Dara stood nearby, panting and sweaty. Despite the carnage around them, seeing her so worked up brought his blood up, and he wanted to ignore the crooning demon before them and take her back to the river. He shook his head and looked away from her and to the bleeding entity.

"Bealzbus," Bel said in greeting, kneeling in the grime and dirt before the vampiric demon. "I did not expect to see you here."

VIII

The fires still burned late into the night. Jojo had approached the human population of the city and given lofty speeches about freedom. He riled them up. They were already fairly agitated. They had seen a dragon. They had seen four beings dismantle and crush one of the oppressor's strongholds. Not only that, they had seen angels bleed. The invincible, the incredible, and the awesome might of the angelic host had been torn apart by the black-scaled giant who now watched over them with glowing orange eyes. They were in awe. But more important than that, they were free. Now a line of humans armed with weapons pillaged from the base was fighting a war they had not known they were part of against a foe they could not imagine. They set up on the edge of the city and slaughtered any of Habbiel's forces that approached from the forest or from the sky. It was a beautiful sight.

Bel turned away from the humans. Bohrm and Dara were directing them, instructing them, turning them into the fighting force they would need to be to avoid being butchered when Habbiel eventually turned his grotesque eyes away from his current degeneracy and brought his gaze upon the rebellion that had been incited. But Bel would be ready for that, or at least he was emotionally ready for that. He wanted to kill a Watcher. He had fought Watchers to a standstill, but in the end, he had been killed by one. His kind had all been killed by Watchers. This new reality in which they could fight the fiends was an exciting one. And not for the first time, Bel reached into the pockets of the pants he wore and pulled the iron railroad spike out. It had runes, and damned spells had been carved into the iron and then inlaid with silver blessed by Kamdiel and Samiel.

According to Lillith and Ashmandai, this could be used to strike the final blow. It was a fetish, invested with all the rage that Kamdiel could muster. It was a totem of the binds that Enoch demanded. It was a prison that would draw in the essence of the fallen Watcher and hold them until such a time that they could truly and permanently be destroyed. There were many such objects, as many as there were Grigori. One for each. Only a few had been used so far, and all of those had been used by Ashmandai or Lillith themselves. He was the first Sheyd other than their Prince and Queen to hold such a relic, to be trusted with it. Bel slipped the iron spike back into his pocket before turning and walking back towards the burning installation.

Jojo was waiting for him. He turned and raised

his eyes to Bel, nodding. "Ready to do this?"

"I am," Bel answered with a grim smile.

Through Bohrm's fantastic shooting, they had taken one of the enemy warriors alive. The demon Bealzbus, an old foe of the Sheydim, a creature who had been on the angelic side of the War since the war began in earnest during the Middle Ages. Bel exhaled a cloud of smoke from his nostrils before nodding, more to himself than to anyone else, and followed Jojo inside one of the few untouched buildings to interrogate their inhuman prisoner.

Inside a cell—little more than a cage—where the angels had been keeping prisoners for fun and torture, Bealzbus sat, leaning against the bars. Bohrm had shot the demon's legs out from under it, a well-placed .50 caliber bullet ripping through the flesh to sever the limbs at the knee. Once, this body, this shell, had been human. Before the essence of Bealzbus had crept in, infecting it. Five arms, two legs, those strange starburst eyes all over its chest, neck, and head, and the jaws that looked like they had been stretched over and then ripped apart by mandibles. Now added to the grotesqueness of their prisoner, pairs of fly wings had sprouted all over its body, each pair beating franticly as though trying to escape their flesh prison. And they probably were. The thousands of wings all moving in unison created a mind numbing buzz that set the teeth on edge.

Bel considered dousing the trapped demon in flames, simply to silence the sound. But killing this body would merely free the demon's essence. Bealzbus was no common spirit but one capable of possessing, mutating, and controlling numerous mortal hosts at a time.

"Hello, Bealzbus," Bel said, crouching in front of the cage that held the demon.

Fourteen bloodshot eyes, all different hues, turned towards him. The buzzing paused for a second before ramping up.

"Bel ... we had heard you were dead. We were sure of it."

"No such luck. Wishful thinking on behalf of your masters," Bel said with a smirk in response.

"Wishful thinking? No, likely more like a logical assumption. I must ask, Bel, I must ask." The demon's chittering was frantic and fast. The sign of panic, or just the manic speech patterns of the stretched-thin thing? "Where were you when your kindred fell? As their blood soaked the ground and fed trees of flesh on my master's ground? Where were you when the dragons went from the most terrifying of Sheydim to whispered forgotten things? From strong and sure to was and were?"

Bel snarled and reached for the cage but was interrupted by Jojo putting a hand on his shoulder. "He's trying to anger you. He wants you to destroy this form, to release him."

Bel fumed but nodded, composing himself.

"What choice do you have? You cannot hurt me in any way that will not cause me pleasure. I have been at the mercy of my sires for millennia."

It was true. Bealzbus had been born from the union between a Sheyd and an angel, less powerful than either but still a strange half-life. What horrors had the creature known? But despite those horrors, it had sided with the angels in this ancient war. Bel had no sympathy.

"We have the means with which to end you, to end your wandering and multiplicity." He removed the iron railroad spike from his pocket and turned it over in his hands. "We have the means to hold you still and remove all distraction and joy from your existences. No pain, no pleasure, nothing but the emptiness of limbo. This will pull all of you into a single point, trapping your entire being in nothingness." Bel smiled now, reveling in the cruelty of it.

The demon scooted back, pressing his body as far away from the spike as he could get. It could sense the power woven into the iron spike, the touch of its master's brother and sister. The old magic that had been worked into the rusted piece of metal. It knew this was no bluff. This was no empty promise. Bel would gladly banish his foe to the nothingness. But still, it blustered. "Such a weapon, but I imagine you have more pressing enemies than a low demon."

"You seem to forget, Bealzbus," Bel said, his voice oozing out of his throat like magma bubbling slowly from the crust of the Earth. "My absence has made you lose sight of who I am. What I want. I want nothing more than to hurt you in a way that truly hurts you, Bealzbus. I want to press my ear to this spike and listen to your echoing wails of bored anguish. But my friend here, he has bigger enemies, he has more important prey than you. It is up to him to convince me not to end your presence in this reality. It is up to you to convince him to convince me."

Bel slid the weapon back in his pocket and stepped away from the cage. "All yours," Bel murmured before leaning against a nearby pillar. He closed his eyes, feigning boredom. He wanted nothing more than to rip the disgusting demon's host apart as he had done on a hundred battlefields before. He held a special hatred for the vampiric demon. The creature was a disease, one that spread throughout humankind and warped them into monstrous things that fed on blood and death. He would kill the thing, but if it played nice with Jojo, then he wouldn't trap its essence first.

Jojo spoke slowly, his voice a whisper, forcing the demon to silence his thousand wings in an attempt to hear the satyr. The rumble of the conversation went back and forth. Each lie that Bealzbus told was answered with a slowly opening orange eye. The creature was not one of subtlety and deceit. It was not clever. Bohrm and Dara entered as Jojo interrogated the creature.

The three were anxious. They had limited time. Human couriers were spreading the news of dissent and rebellion to every corner of Habbiel's kingdom. Across the island, cities and settlements of humans were turning their minds from mindless and fearful subservience to resentful rage. They were arming; they were taking back their island from the horrors of the Grigori. But this also meant that they only had moments to spare. Soon word of this would reach the Watcher. And then the Watcher would come for them. The lesser angels and demons were nothing compared to the flesh-shaping fragments of original creation, the true angels that had fallen. Bohrm moved to stand next to Jojo, but Dara moved to Bel and sat next to him, leaning her head against his leg.

Exhausted, unable to resist any longer, Bealzbus held up a hand. It may love the pain, but the loss of blood had turned to shock, driving him to numbness and hunger, draining the world of color. Finally, he spoke of Habbiel's fortress, its defenses, and, most importantly, its entrances. Jojo stepped back and nodded to Bel. Bel shook his leg, dislodging the succubus as he stepped forward and exhaled a massive fireball that swallowed the demon. Its skin popped and fizzed as it cooked. The demon's hundred eyes melted in their sockets, running down its body like cheese in an oven. The three of them watched, deaf to its suffering, as it burned down to nothing, even the bones consumed in the conflagration of Bel's supernatural dragon fire. When there was nothing left but a greasy spot inside the still locked cage, Bel turned towards the door.

"Come, we have a Watcher to kill."

IX.

The four of them left the facility, picking their way around the flaming wreckage of equipment that Dara had destroyed.

"Did you have to blow up every fucking vehicle?" Bohrm asked.

"You wanted chaos, I gave you chaos," she answered easily, tossing a grenade over her shoulder and into the building they had left.

"Yes, but now we need a way to get to Habbiel's fortress. You may have forgotten that not all of us can fly."

"Shut up, Bohrm," Jojo grunted. "But he is right, Dara, we need to find some way to travel quickly. If we try to hoof it there, we'll be sitting ducks for Habbiel's forces."

Dara stuck her tongue out at Jojo but looked around, obviously considering the predicament.

Bel was less worried. If he needed to, he would abandon the small team and fly to Habbiel's fortress on his own. But would the three of them survive without him? Within the hour, Bel surmised, the forces of Habbiel would begin converging on them. The angel's many eyes would be focused on them. They could no longer hide. While Bel didn't feel he needed to include this rag-tag bunch in the fight just to make them feel validated, he didn't want them to die. Jojo was a capable leader and fighter, even Bohrm had proven himself a deadly asset with his long range rifle. Dara was … Dara had her uses too, and he was fond of her, though he didn't know if that fondness was entirely his or if it was her nature as a succubus to pull at him. He would need to discuss this with the queen, or even Agrat, they would know more of the intricacies of the succubi than any other. But even if the three of them were useless, he had been asked by his King and Queen to watch over them. Whatever other thoughts or misgivings he might have, he would return them to the City alive.

"There!" Dara shouted, interrupting Bel's train of thought.

He followed her finger as she pointed towards a large, sturdy-looking flatbed truck. Bel didn't know much about these contraptions. They had not existed when he was put into his deathly sleep, and so far as he could tell, no one in the City-East-of-Nod used them. Could such a massive machine actually get them to their destination faster than the power of their own feet? He would have to trust that his teammates knew what they were doing and what they were talking about. Easier said than done.

"Bel and Dara, take the back; Bohrm you're

in the cab with me," Jojo ordered as he tossed their supplies onto the back of the truck. He then clambered into the front and began fiddling with something.

Bel watched, bemused, unsure what was happening, when suddenly the thing roared to life. It was a low growl of motors and machinery, which startled him. He regained his composure quickly, glad neither Bohrm nor Jojo had witnessed his start.

"What was that?" her voice was playful, but Bel's mind interpreted it as mocking and he turned towards Dara with a snarl. Her eyes widened in surprise for a moment and then narrowed in anger. "I don't know who the fuck you think you're making angry faces at, but I'm not the one, Bel." She let that threat, empty as it might be, hang in the air. Tension growing.

He considered her words, her ideas. He tried to put himself in her shoes but could not, they were not merely different species but of wildly different time periods.

"Just because we fucked, just because I enjoy you, does not give you ownership of me, it doesn't give you permission to ever, *ever*," she stressed, hissing the word, "treat me with anything other than respect. You fucking understand that?"

He slowly nodded, his orange eyes glowing

as he controlled his own rage at being spoken to this way. She wildly misunderstood him if she thought that he wanted to own her or felt any possessiveness towards her. But that was fair; she didn't know him, and he didn't know her. Outside of the biblical sense.

"Likewise, I expect to be treated with respect too. I do not appreciate being mocked." He stated it simply and turned back towards the truck, stepping past her to pull himself up. He looked down at her, watching the confusion and then realization cross her face.

"Wait," she said, leaping up and joining him on the back of the truck. "You felt like I was mocking you by asking why you jumped? You need to can that bullshit immediately. Don't be so sensitive. I saw you rip an angel apart with your bare hands and eat it, and it was fucking hot. But hotness aside, it was powerful, primal, brutal, so I think I can ask why a truck starting made you jump." She sat and pulled her RPG launcher into her lap as they started to move.

Bel watched her. She was a strange one. Brutality and power aroused her but disrespect would make her square up against a far superior combatant. She watched him, waiting for some explanation. She still had that grim set to her jaw; the tension was still there. He considered ignoring her, he owed her nothing, just as she owed him nothing. But he wanted her focused on the mission of destroying the Watcher, not on him.

"Agrat told me about vehicles and cars. But I had not seen one before I came here. I was not expecting the sound," he said bluntly.

Dara watched him, her eyes narrowed, her cute upturned nose crinkled, as if she were suspicious of his honesty. After a moment, though, she nodded. "Okay, well, if you're sorry for growling at me like an asshole, I'm sorry for snapping at you."

She watched him as though waiting for him to respond. He didn't. He was sure she expected him to apologize or to launch into some long explanation of the world he came from and the world he woke up to. But he didn't have the patience for it. He had one purpose and one purpose only: the destruction of Watchers. If she believed the sex they had shared would lead to him being a source of food and power for her, she was mistaken.

He nodded, so as not to ignore her statement entirely, and turned his blazing eyes to the sky, where he suspected an attack from Habbiel would be forthcoming.

X.

After an hour, Dara suddenly spoke, shattering his silent vigil. "It's beautiful, isn't it?"

Bel glanced at the succubus. She was beautiful for a warm blood. Her electric blue hair glimmered in the setting sun. Her caramel skin seemed to shine and shimmer where the light kissed her. She was lithe and strong, a survivor. Despite her carefree attitude, her life, the life of every Sheydim, had been war. War unending. It made for strong people. He looked past her at the way the golden and red light of the sinking sun reflected off the big waxy leaves of the jungle trees.

"Yes," he finally answered. "It is beautiful. It reminds me of home."

"Home?" she asked, turning her face from the sun to look at him. "You don't mean the City …"

"The City-East-Of-Nod was not always my home, no. And it was never my main home. No, I had a villa, an estate near an oasis in Egypt. They called me Sobek in those days, and while much of Egypt was swallowed by the sands and dunes, there were lush oases, places of life and vitality. And it was beautiful in this way." He wondered if his estate still stood or if it had been swallowed by the desert the way so much of his life had been subsumed by tragedy. Even if it did still stand, humans would have found it and moved in. It was as lost to him as any of the past few hundred years.

He was about to go on when Dara suddenly leapt to her feet, slinging the RPG to her shoulder. "We have incoming!" she shouted.

Bel looked over his shoulder at where she was aiming and indeed saw the shapes of humanoids with wings spread wide flying right towards them. Bel rose as well, stumbling a little as he worked to gain his balance on the moving vehicle. Dara took a knee and aimed through her scope before letting loose with a rocket.

Her aim was true, and the explosion left a golden cloud of falling feathers in its wake. But there were more. Many more. Bel moved to the supply bag and sifted through it, trying to remember which gun did what. Finally, he chose one of the longer guns—a rifle, if memory served—and turned to face the incoming angels.

He had wondered if he would go this entire mission without once getting to sample the true destructive power of these weapons. The weight of it in his hands felt unreal; it felt too light to be deadly, too complicated to be reliable. But he had seen first-hand what these weapons could do as Dara and Bohrm had unleashed them. Now it was his turn. He brought the weapon to his shoulder, aimed at the nearest angel, and squeezed the trigger.

The rifle kicked against him, but it was no match for his strength. He kept it steady and true. And missed. Badly. Despite his training at Agrat's firing range, he was ill prepared to fire an assault rifle off the back of a moving truck at moving targets that were so far away. Dara touched his shoulder and pulled the rifle from his hands. She offered him just one sympathetic smile before turning and snapping off a shot.

She had done this before. Though she missed a few of the shots, the angels were now forced to take evasive maneuvers to avoid being shot. She also couldn't shoot all of them.

Bel turned, irritated. He could take wing and take the fight to the angels, but should any slip past him, they would land on the truck and may hurt or even kill Dara. That would not do. He turned back towards the supply bag and pulled it open. It was magical in its own right, sturdy beyond what should be possible and much, much larger on the inside than on the outside. Bel's eyes traveled over the armory of weapons, both ranged and melee. He found what he was looking for and grabbed two large khopesh swords from the bag. He turned around just in time to see the first angels landing on the back of the truck. Dara was backing up and cursing as more angels landed.

"Eyes on the sky Chaos-Bringer," he chided as he stepped past her to meet the angels. Dara didn't have to be told twice, returning her aim to the targets still in the air. "Come purpose-breakers and rape-happy pigeons. I am Sobek of the Nile, Cipactli the Devourer, I am Jörmungandr, Leviathan, Typhon. I earned worship from the humans before your masters came and demanded what was not theirs."

The angels, feral creatures of twisted divinity and deranged purpose, knew no fear. They had not been designed to understand it.

Bel would be their instructor, and their lessons would be brief. He sprang forward, the mighty curved swords slashing out. One angel managed to dodge out of the way, the other was caught. The sword slammed through its shoulder and cleanly chopped through the torso, rocketing out of the angel's body through the opposite hip. Golden blood splattered the truck, and the two parts of the angel fell tumbling off the back of the vehicle. The smell of the divine blood sent the surviving angel into a frenzy, and it was just the vanguard of a swarm that was descending on them.

Without pausing to consider the danger they were in, Bel pressed his attack He stepped forward and planted a hard kick in the angel's chest, sending it backwards. His swords were already coming up over his head and slashing down so that as the angel spread its wings to catch itself, they were severed. The creature howled in agony as it crashed back down to the earth and was left in the dust behind the moving truck.

He couldn't relish the moment as more were landing, drawing golden blades, the trappings of nobility in debased disgusting creatures. Bel was unimpressed. Dara was screaming in battle lust. She had moved to the supply bag and grabbed some terrifying gun with a dozen barrels that spun around spitting death into the air with a high, horrible whine. Golden blood rained down on them from the heavens.

Bel did not stop moving, moving as though he danced through his enemies, each twist of his wrist and snap of a leg making contact with the damned flock of unholy attackers. It seemed these angels were never ending, but Bel understood what they were, made not by the Creator but by the Watchers themselves. Sacrificing their own divinity, shaping reality in order to create servants in a shape that was both familiar and pleasing to them. There would be virtually no end to the servile parrots that were flitting around waiting for their turn at a messy death.

Bel spun into a kneeling position, blades

outstretched to hew legs from bodies as he opened his mouth wide and let loose with a gout of dragon fire. The blast of heat scorched a clear space on the back of the truck, flaming angelic corpses falling to either side of the vehicle as it powered on. Rising, Bel met the swords of the next angel with his own, parrying the attack before spinning to block another angel's descending axe. He twisted his wrist, disarming the first angel, bringing his blocking sword back around to punch through that angel's chest before he ripped the blade out the side and turned to bite into the other angel's throat and rip his trachea out.

There was a thrum in the air. A bass note that vibrated atmosphere. Bel could feel it just beneath the motor and wheels; it was everywhere and growing stronger. The angels were hanging back, now focused solely on avoiding Dara's Gatling gun. But she couldn't feel the danger over the vibration of her own gun.

Bel turned to her. "Get down!" he roared, trying to be heard over the atonal drone filling the air and the scream of her weapon.

Dara didn't hear him, and even if she had, it was too late. A green light filled the air. The droning became so loud, so overpowering that it eclipsed all other sounds and experiences. Something hit the truck with the force of a comet.

The flatbed flew apart under the impact, the metal screaming as it twisted violently and shattered. Dara was thrown as the truck bent in the middle like plastic in the hands of an angry toddler, and her body ragdolled into the surrounding jungle. The front of the truck was carried by momentum and torsion to the side, spinning as it went crashing into the thick foliage. Only Bel remained unmoved, his claws dug into the metal, close enough to the impact to stay put.

From the hole in the ground rose a figure, tall, terrible, and imperious. She was draped in sheer green fabrics that clung to a body that shifted and moved under the garment like a chaotic sea. Between her small pert breasts, a shard of golden darkness that drank in the light sat suspended in a wire amulet. Behind her, four black wings covered in rotting, shimmering feathers stretched out in horrible, unnatural majesty.

Habbiel had arrived.

XI

Against Habbiel, all other beings seemed … less than. She, he, it, they was a fragment of the divine will that shaped all of creation. They were a spark of the divine sundered from holy purpose by malicious intent. Purity-of-being traded for purity-of-purpose. There had been a time, at the very beginning of it all, when the Sheydim had thought the Watchers and they were kindred. Things tossed aside by the Creator. Entities bent on forging their own paths away from the light and rule of authority to reality for realms of self-expression and knowledge.

How wrong they were. The Grigori, Habbiel themself, was an emissary of authority and tyranny. A creature of cruel desires who believed all of creation existed for their own sordid pleasure. The Grigori were in many ways the Sheydim's mirror opposite. They desired nothing but full and utter control over all things. They warped all around them to their own liking, their own vision of creation. They were without mercy or remorse, as close to gods as an entity could be.

Bel kept no space for fear in his heart as he watched the Grigori take stock of the damage around them. He flicked his twin blades, slinging golden blood from the weapons. "Come to join your flock in death, Watcher?" He spoke the ancient language of Sumer.

"Death. I am beyond death, beyond the reach of little shades of Sheydim." They towered over Bel in his human form, nine feet of dark glory.

"And yet I have reached you." Bel sneered as he took three steps forward and swiped at the Watcher with a three-strike combo.

The angel shrunk and grew, their body warping to be just out of the way of each strike. He leapt back as Habbiel counterattacked with a back hand of their own. He landed ten feet back. The world shifted. The back of Habbiel's hand came into contact with Bel's cheek as he was suddenly standing two feet from them.

The blow sent him hurtling through the air, tumbling end over end. He hit the ground amongst the shrapnel left by the Watcher's arrival and rolled several meters, only to land at Habbiel's feet.

"Killing little things has made you cocky, lizard. But I am not a fraction, I am a whole. And even at your best, you are a half." Habbiel lifted their foot and brought it down to stomp out this impetuous reptile.

Bel rose at the same time, bringing his shoulder up and into the Watcher. They gasped, the air knocked out of lungs they had formed simply to taunt him as they were knocked back and off balance.

They were weaker than they expected to be, slower, their dominion disintegrating around them as rebellion bubbled up across the island. Yet they were still Grigori, still far more powerful than any other. Catching themself, they peered at Bel, perhaps with new appreciation but more likely with the curiosity of a child who had caught a stinging insect.

"We know you. You were dead. Dead at the head of a thousand half-bred reptiles who plummeted towards doom in your wake. You are their father, their gold tongued serpent who whispered in the ear of the whisperer long before Adam met Eve. I know you, Bel, first of the dragons."

Habbiel seemed pleased with themself for identifying Bel.

Bel, for his part, pressed on, pushing forward and swinging his swords, attempting to find any purchase in Grigori flesh. "First, last, alpha, omega—I am not some worshipful mortal who gapes at your knowledge, Watcher," he hissed as he continued to strike at air, the Watcher's shifting of reality denying him a clean strike on them.

"You should worship, all should worship. There is a place at my feet for the strong. These islands are ours, lizard, they are ours to command and change as we see fit!" With those words, Habbiel raised their hand. The trees surrounding them morphed into fleshy tendrils coated in seeping skin, writhing in the ground, reaching for Bel.

Bel did not let up his assault. If the Watcher wished to strike him, they would need to stay still for a moment, they would need to be solid enough to land such a strike. That was his hope, but Habbiel seemed happy to toy with their prey. They rose into the sky, out of the reach of Bel's human form. He leapt for them. A skin tendril weeping pus whipped out, catching his leg, and threw him down. The impact was jarring, but Bel continued to rise; he would shift, take his true form and rip this divine atrocity apart tooth and claw. He pushed himself to his knee when a second tendril lashed out, wrapping around one of his arms. It was followed by another, and another, each one pulling him, forcing him down.

Bel's eyes glowed fiercely with an internal orange light, his rage mounting as he pulled in his willpower to assume his true nature. His bones shifted and moved inside him ... or, they attempted to, but he was locked in place, locked into the shape of this scaleless, useless human. A seventh flesh tendril, this one covered in coarse hair and gibbering mandible-bearing mouths, wrapped around his throat, biting and squeezing. He angled his head up at Habbiel, who floated above him, a cruel smirk on their face.

If he could breathe in, he could let loose with dragon fire, burn these tendrils to nothing. But he couldn't, he couldn't get in even the slightest gasp of air. He tried to concentrate. He was Sheyd, he could become immaterial. But Habbiel's power had him firmly anchored in their reality. Or maybe it was this place. Bel didn't worry about being able to breathe, he wasn't mortal, he could go without air. But he could not speak, he could not defend himself.

"You have created a hardship for me, on my island. You have turned the mortals and the little demons against me." Habbiel floated down. Their feet, covered in eyes and moaning mouths, touched down on the ground, corrupted darkness spreading forth from where they made contact. "I will wipe this place clean. As the Creator wiped the earth of my children, so will I cleanse this place and start anew. All you have accomplished, lizard, is to rack up quite a delicious cost in life."

The Watcher reached forward, their hands thick, veiny, bulging with new growth. The corrupting nature of the Watcher's essence was a cancer that he could feel grasping towards him, eager to change him, to remake him.

"The prince sends his greetings, bitch," Dara spat, appearing behind Habbiel. Her blue hair was dirty and matted with sticks and debris; her face scratched and bleeding, one eye swollen shut. Without any other warning, Dara plunged a blade into the side of Habbiel's neck and ripped out the front of their throat.

Hot golden blood splashed across Bel's face. But Bel didn't even blink as the knife that Dara used to cut Habbiel's throat glowed with strange blue runes. They pulled something from the Watcher's body. It was a sickly green mist that crackled with golden lightning as it was sucked into the knife. The drone that had accompanied Habbiel rose in pitch and intensity, a screaming roar that nearly burst their ears. Dara staggered back, gripping the knife with both hands, trying to control it as the Grigori was sucked into its prison. Her hair was blown back and she struggled to maintain her hold.

The flesh coils that held Bel loosened, dying and rotting in a terrible parody of the natural order. As he was freed from their embrace, Bel jumped to brace Dara, his hands wrapping over hers and steadying them both. Through her hands, he could feel the awesome power of the Watcher Habbiel being chained to the essence of the blade.

And then it was over.

Habbiel's body lie in a pool of shit and piss; though grossly inhuman, it had died the way all biological bodies die. The essence of what made it inhuman, what made it divine, was trapped in a knife that was nearly indistinguishable from any other ritualistic tool of murder. Slowly, the drone of their green light that had filled the sky dissipated.

Bel released Dara and staggered forward. He hurt. He now noticed cuts and bruises from his fight, not only against Habbiel but the angels beforehand, that he had not taken stock of during the battle.

He reached down and ripped the amulet from the still cooling corpse and held it up. It was Kelipot, a shard of the original shattered word of creation, an inky blackness trapped beneath a glowing golden wire that was powered by cruelty and malice. Only through cleansing it would the world to come ever be unleashed.

"What the hell?" Bohrm called as he and Jojo crested the hill and looked over the carrion field of rotting phallic flesh-trees.

Dara gave him a lop-sided grin as she pocketed the knife, the grim strength she had displayed moments ago now hidden once again. "You missed all the fun, is what the hell. Mission accomplished." She gestured towards the dead Watcher.

Jojo nodded as he joined them. "I knew you could do it, Bel."

Bel was about to correct the satyr about who

had dealt the final blow when Dara interrupted him. "Yup, it was pretty amazing to watch. I'm lucky I decided not to hide like a couple of bitches!"

"Hide! I wasn't hiding!" Bohrm shouted. "We got knocked nearly half a kilometer away. We've been running the entire fucking way back."

Jojo shook his head as the two fell into bickering playfully. "Time for me to send you all home," he said, pulling a rod of red stone from his belt.

"Send us?" Bel asked.

"Yeah. I'll stay behind, help clean up whatever loyalist filth is left, help the mortals establish some form of government. You know, nature abhors a power vacuum. I'm sure the City will send me some bureaucratic help, but for now ..."

"I would be no help in those matters," Bel finished for him.

Jojo nodded. "You've earned rest." He raised the rod in his hand and rapped it against a bracelet around his forearm that had been hidden by his coat before. For several moments, nothing happened. The battlefield was filled with the sound of buzzing flies and Dara exaggerating the fight to Bohrm. Bel watched the two of them; they reminded him of siblings, which in turn reminded him of his siblings, all dead now, all bone and ash. Before he could slip into a further melancholy, a shimmering red portal opened in the air before

Jojo. Through the rend in reality, Bel could just make out the towers and facades of the City-East-of-Nod.

Without a word to the others, or even a thank you to Jojo, Bel turned and strode through the portal to return to the place he now called home.

XII

Their return home was met with fanfare and jubilee. It was a celebration on par with that to which Bel had awoken almost a year ago. If anything, it was more animated. There was more celebration, more fights, more sex, more chaos. Two of the Watchers had been ended within a year of one another. The long war was changing, it was coming. By now, the entire City had learned of the returning hero, Bel. And hardly a soul, demon or Sheyd, had missed Dara's version of the fight, which spread through the City with a life of its own.

The night of the celebration, fireworks lit the sky and wild magic illuminated nearly every surface as life, victory, and, most importantly, freedom was venerated. Lillith had sparked this war, but it was a natural conflict. The Grigori were tyrants who demanded complete control over all things. The Sheydim were agents of free will and self-expression. And tonight, both of those things were on full display. Art displays, music, theater, dramatic readings—all of it flooded the streets.

Banquets with foods from all over the globe, both natural and supernatural taverns and cafes, and all the shop doors, and even the doors to the castle, were thrown open for visitors. Even Jojo and his team of administrators had come back for the night, taking a break from stabilizing the region to enjoy the fruits of their labors. Speeches were made, toasts were drunk, and tears of joy and pride were freely shed.

Only Bel was missing the festivities.

In his room in the palace, Bel wrapped himself in the fine robes that Lillith had gifted him. He appreciated all these things that the Sheydim celebrated, but he was not one for huge crowds and formal events. He did not care about glory or praise. He stood in front of a bust of some Sheyd hero, carved in the third century CE. One of the few treasures of Bel's hoard that Ashmandai had seen fit to bring to the palace. After several minutes, Bel placed the Kelipot amulet he had ripped from Habbiel's corpse around the neck of the bust. His first new acquisition in centuries.

"Not in the mood for a party?" Dara asked from the doorway. "They're moving your statue from the garden of remembrance. You aren't dead, so I guess they figure you deserve to be someplace for the living." She was leaning against the doorstop. In her hands, she carried two hot dogs, an offering. She was dressed in a simple white sundress that was quite complimentary to her shape, her electric blue hair loose and wavy, catching the low light of his room in scintillating patterns.

He glanced at her, weighing how she had managed to get into the palace and find him versus how he felt about her interrupting his solitude. Dara didn't interrupt his contemplation, seeming at ease with the slow speed at which he took his thoughts. Bel's tongue flicked out catching the scents in the air; those hot dogs smelled delicious. After a moment, he decided maybe he didn't mind her intrusion. Besides, he had a question.

"Why don't you claim the glory? You struck the killing blow, you took the Watcher's life, all of," he waved his hand to indicate the noise and celebratory sounds coming from outside the walls, "should be for you."

Dara shrugged and took his question as an invitation to step inside his room. She didn't answer right away as she looked over his hoard, her eyes traveling over treasures that few Sheydim, and even fewer mortal eyes, had ever fallen on. "Belief is a powerful thing, especially when you think about the Watchers. I'm just a soldier, a succubus, a nobody." She turned to face Bel, approaching him and offering him one of the hot dogs. He took it. "You're already a legend. You've returned from the dead, you've already fought the Watchers. I don't care about being a hero or being famous or anything like that."

"Neither do I," Bel protested quietly between

bites.

"Right, I know, but I didn't do it for you. I did it for them, for my people, for the City. You're going to be called on to hunt these Grigori down. They need to have faith in you, they need heroes that aren't Lord Ashmandai or Queen Lillith. They need to be excited about winning. And you can do that, or at least the idea of you can do that. That's why I lied."

"Lord Ashmandai, the queen, and Agrat all know the truth," Bel reminded her.

"Yes, and you'll notice they haven't done anything to correct the circulating stories. They know that propaganda and morale is as important and potent a weapon in this war as anything else. Even you know that."

Bel grunted; he knew she was right, even if he didn't like it.

"I just wanted to check on you, Bel." She crumpled her empty napkin as she finished her meal. "And maybe bring you some good food, maybe see if you needed some company." She reached out and touched his chest, slowly drawing a circle on his skin with her fingertip.

He finished his own food and looked down at her. He had been enjoying his solitude, but the food and the company was surprisingly refreshing and invigorating. He didn't ask what she meant, he reached around her and pulled her closer, pressing his body against hers. She was warm and supple.

Dara reached up, wrapping her arms around Bel's neck, pulling him down. Her lips met his just a moment before she bit his lower lip. She pulled back, offering him a devious grin. "Not too gentle now," she commanded, releasing him and moving towards his bed.

Bel followed, already reaching forward to tear her dress off.

John Baltisberger

John Baltisberger is an author of speculative and genre fiction that often focuses on Jewish Elements. Beyond his writing career, John is the Publishing Editor of Madness Heart Press, Madness Heart Games, and Aggadah Try It.

A fan of transgressive and experimental literature. He lives with his wife, daughter and trash-goblin/pug Beans in Austin, Texas. You can see his work and more at www.KaijuPoet.com

More Books from John Baltisberger

From Madness Heart Press;

UPD, Texas Case Files: 1.1-1.3
978-1-955745-01-7

From Aggadah Try It;

Book of Ze'ev: Treif Magic
978-1-7348937-0-0

Book of Ze'ev: Son of the Right Hand
978-1-955745-04-8

From St. Rooster Books;

Abhorrent Siren
978-1-955745-02-4

Aborrent Faith
978-1-955745-09-3

Blood & Mud
979-8647568397

From Death's Head Press;

War of Dictates
978-1-7348937-1-7

More Kaiju Press Publications;

Stabberger Season One
978-1-955745-12-3

The Subjective Truth of the Esoteric Mind
978-1-7348937-2-4